"Who are you?" she asked.

"I told you, I'm Cole Grayson."

"That's not what I mean. They've been calling me Jane Doe. That might even be my name, or maybe it's Susan Smith or Mary Jackson. But whatever it is, a name doesn't tell anything about who I am or who you are."

He gazed down at her for a long moment then finally turned away and angled a hip onto the windowsill, studying their reflection in the dark glass. "I'm nobody you want to know."

A gray veil of desolation emanated from him. She could see it, feel it in the weight of the air, smell the leaden scent, taste the bitter agony. Perhaps because her mind was completely empty of her own emotions, his came to her, strong and clear.

"I don't have a choice right now," she said. "You're the only person I know."

Dear Harlequin Intrigue Reader,

The recipe for a perfect Valentine's Day: chocolate, champagne—and four original romantic suspense titles from Harlequin Intrigue!

Our TOP SECRET BABIES promotion kicks off with Rita Herron's *Saving His Son* (#601). Devastated single mother Lindsey Payne suspects her child is alive and well— and being kept from her deliberately. The only man who'd be as determined as she is to find her child is Detective Gavin McCord—*if* he knew he'd fathered her missing baby....

In *Best-Kept Secrets* (#602) by Dani Sinclair, the tongues in MYSTERY JUNCTION are wagging about newcomer Jake Collins. Amy Thomas's first and only love has returned at last and she's ready to tell him the secret she's long kept hidden. But would revealing it suddenly put her life in jeopardy?

Our ON THE EDGE program continues with *Private Vows* (#603) by Sally Steward. A beautiful amnesiac is desperate to remember her past. Investigator Cole Grayson is desperate to keep it hidden. For if she remembers the truth, she'd never be his....

Bachelor Will Sheridan thinks he's found the perfect *Mystery Bride* (#604) in B.J. Daniels's latest romantic thriller. But the sexy and provocative Samantha Murphy is a female P.I. in the middle of a puzzling case when Will suddenly becomes her shadow. Now with desire distracting her and a child's life in the balance, Samantha and Will are about to discover the true meaning of "partnership"!

Next month more from TOP SECRET BABIES and ON THE EDGE, plus a 3-in-1 collection from some of your favorite authors and the launch of Sheryl Lynn's new McCLINTOCK COUNTRY miniseries.

Sincerely,

Denise O'Sullivan
Associate Senior Editor
Harlequin Intrigue

PRIVATE VOWS
SALLY STEWARD

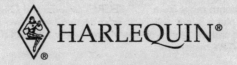

HARLEQUIN®

TORONTO • NEW YORK • LONDON
AMSTERDAM • PARIS • SYDNEY • HAMBURG
STOCKHOLM • ATHENS • TOKYO • MILAN • MADRID
PRAGUE • WARSAW • BUDAPEST • AUCKLAND

ISBN 0-373-22603-9

PRIVATE VOWS

Copyright © 2001 by Sally B. Steward.

This edition published by arrangement with Harlequin Books S.A.

® and TM are trademarks of the publisher. Trademarks indicated with
® are registered in the United States Patent and Trademark Office, the
Canadian Trade Marks Office and in other countries.

Visit us at www.eHarlequin.com

Printed in U.S.A.

ABOUT THE AUTHOR

Sally Steward, a hard-core romantic who expects life and novels to have happy endings, is married to Max and they live in Missouri, with their large cat, Leo, and their very small dog, Cricket. Although this is her first Harlequin Intrigue, Sally has written for mainstream publishers under her own name, and for Silhouette Romance as Sally Carleen. Her hobbies are drinking Coca-Cola and eating chocolate, especially Ben & Jerry's Phish Food ice cream. Sally loves to hear from her readers, and you can contact her at P.O. Box 6614, Lee's Summit, MO 64064.

Books by Sally Steward

HARLEQUIN INTRIGUE
603—PRIVATE VOWS

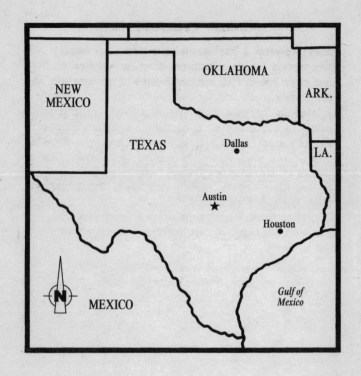

CAST OF CHARACTERS

Cole Grayson—The former-cop-turned-private-investigator wants to help the beautiful woman with amnesia but fears he will only lead her straight to hell.

Mary Jackson—She can't remember anything from her past except for vague, terrifying images, images that fit with the blood on her wedding gown.

Pete Townley—The police officer is skeptical of Mary's story. Does she really have amnesia or is she covering up a deadly secret?

Sam Maynard—He claims to be Mary's fiancé. He's obsessed with her, has his bedroom plastered with her pictures.

Geoffrey Sloan—He's wealthy, charming and handsome and also says he's Mary's fiancé....

For Sharon Bishop.

Chapter One

With the top down on his big old T-bird convertible and one arm angled out the window, Cole Grayson drove slowly along Turtle Creek Boulevard, focusing on the trees and flowers, breathing in their essence, breathing out the bad taste his last job had left with him. This wasn't the fastest way home by any means, but the older, wooded area—so close to downtown Dallas in actual mileage but so distant in other ways—always soothed him.

The early-June evening and the location were perfect, but they weren't working their magic, weren't dissolving that edgy, irritable feeling. He sat upright in the seat, fingers clenching the steering wheel, eyes darting from side to side, glowering at other drivers, ready to lean on the horn if somebody committed a slight infraction. What the hell was the matter with him? He should be happy!

He'd just turned in his final report on his last job, helping a large corporation catch an embezzler. Last month he'd found proof of fraud in an insurance scam. Business was booming, and it was good business. It paid better than being a cop and was certainly less dangerous.

And he felt totally useless.

Up ahead a woman emerged from between two buildings and paused, looking up and down the street. Cole sat even straighter and blinked, doubting his own eyes.

The woman wore a formal bridal gown.

Her clothing alone was enough to make him take notice, but it was her face, pale in the gathering dusk, her eyes wide with fear, that really caught his attention.

His foot jerked off the gas pedal and hovered over the brake but he ordered himself to go on. This was none of his business. He wasn't a cop any longer and hadn't been a very effective one when he was. The woman didn't appear to be hurt. There was no reason for him to interfere.

A shabbily dressed man approached her and laid a hand on her arm. She screamed and whirled on the man, pummeling him with both fists. He tried to grab her hands, but she bolted into the street, directly in front of Cole's car, the inappropriate yards of satin and lace billowing around her as she moved.

Cole slammed the brake pedal to the floor. His stomach lurched and a cold hand squeezed his heart as he felt and heard the sickening thud when over a ton of metal collided with a hundred pounds of flesh and bone.

The bride and all her regalia vanished from sight, hidden by the hood of his car.

He vaulted into the street, cursing himself, the woman, the man who'd frightened her…the world.

She lay on her stomach, almost hidden by the folds and layers of that damn frilly material.

Cole knelt beside her and picked up her arm encased in a lacy sleeve fastened with a bunch of little buttons.

His big fingers trembled as he wrapped them around her slim wrist, searching for a pulse while his own pounded in his ears and made hers that much harder to distinguish.

He'd been a cop for twelve years. He ought to be used to this kind of thing.

But he wasn't and he hadn't been even when he lived with it on a daily basis.

He found her pulse, weak and fast as though she was in shock…or the terror he'd seen on her face still gripped her, but at least she was alive. Thank God he'd been going slow, that he'd already been poised to brake.

"Is she okay?" a man asked. Not the street person who'd scared her but a jogger, his face damp with perspiration.

"There's a cell phone in my car! Call 911. Hurry!"

A small crowd of half a dozen people was starting to gather around them—concerned citizens, curiosity seekers.

The bride moaned and moved as if she was going to turn over. Well, she couldn't be very comfortable with her face shoved into the street.

"Easy," he cautioned. "Try not to move until the ambulance gets here."

She gave no indication she even heard him, but rolled slowly and languidly, one arm flung above her head, as though she were turning over in her bed at home. She gazed up at him, light blue eyes blank in shock, not yet registering her situation.

She blinked then. Confusion surfaced and finally the fear again, her pupils shrinking to a pinpoint, the surrounding blue so pale it appeared almost silver in its translucence.

"No!" she choked, pushing herself into a sitting position, and he saw for the first time that the front of the dress was splattered with blood—lots of blood.

Cole broke into a sweat as the image of another woman, covered in blood because of him, flashed across the screen of his memory.

The woman in the bridal gown scooted away from him...toward the traffic in the street.

"Damn it, lady!" He grabbed her arm to pull her back, to keep her from further injury, and she burst into tears, collapsing against him.

"Let me go! Please let me go!" she begged.

Much as he'd like to do just that, let her go and pretend the whole thing never happened, he couldn't. Instead, he held her as securely as he dared, considering the extent of the wound he must have caused.

"You're going to be all right," he assured her, though he wasn't certain that she would be with all that blood on her dress. "That bum who was bothering you is gone." The guy was probably harmless enough and her reaction to him had been, Cole thought, a little over the top, but he'd say whatever necessary to reassure her.

He stroked her back soothingly, the roughness of his palms snagging on the smooth satin. Her clean, innocent scent of lily-of-the-valley or some other white flower drifted up to him, cutting through the smell of hot pavement. She was thin and fragile, as if she would snap from too tight a grip.

Again that image of a broken doll, broken because of him, assaulted him.

Damn! This shouldn't be happening. For the twelve years he'd been a cop he'd had no problem dealing with murderers and thieves and drug dealers, looking them in the eye and backing them down without even breathing hard. But this was asking too much, to expect him to cope with a terrified, fragile woman. He couldn't. He'd long ago proven that.

"Lie back," he ordered brusquely.

"No, no, no!" Face still buried against his chest, she shook her head, the netting of her veil shivering with the movement.

"There's blood on your dress. I need to see how badly you're hurt." Reminding himself that she was in shock, he spoke more softly, made an effort not to startle her.

She continued to shake her head and cry.

He gripped her thin shoulders and pushed her away, forcing her to look at him. "Listen to me! I'm not going to hurt you. But you need to let me examine your wound."

A woman from the group of onlookers knelt beside her. "Let me see, honey. Okay?"

Her tears stopping as if something inside had turned off, the bride gave the woman a puzzled glance then lifted her gaze to the chattering group around her as though she'd suddenly noticed her surroundings, suddenly woke up.

"The front of her dress," Cole directed, and the woman nodded, gently turning the now-pliant bride to face her.

"Oh my God!" the woman exclaimed when she saw the crimson stains.

The bride's gaze followed the other woman's, and she gasped, then lifted her eyes to his again. Those eyes were even wider and more confused than ever, more frightened.

Now that Cole had a better look at the blood, he saw

with a rush of relief that it was not coming from a fresh wound, nor was her gown torn. Either it had come from a preexisting wound or from somebody else. Not from her. Not from a wound caused by him.

Had she cut the man who'd approached her?

Automatically he rose to investigate the sidewalk where she and the man had been before she'd run into the street, to check for blood or a weapon.

"Don't leave me!"

A hand gripped his arm with surprising strength and he turned to see the bride struggling to her feet. She was tall, which only emphasized her slender build, and she swayed as if she might not be able to stand without his support.

On the positive side, the fact that she was able to stand at all meant she couldn't be hurt too badly. He clung to that, to the faint hope that he hadn't caused her any permanent harm.

"A minute ago you were doing your damnedest to get away from me," he reminded her.

"I know." She released his arm and lifted both hands to her face. Hesitantly her slim fingers traced its tear-stained contours as if she'd never felt them before. "I mean, I don't know. I don't know why I wanted to get away from you. Who are you?"

"Cole Grayson. Who are you?"

She touched her face again. When her fingers encountered the edge of the veil, she frowned, fumbled for a second then yanked it off, releasing a cascade of quicksilver-blond hair. She studied the veil, turning it over as if secrets were hidden in its gauzy folds, looked down at the bloody gown then back up at him. The fear in her eyes had escalated to panic and spots of pink stood out on her porcelain cheeks like clown makeup. "I don't know," she whispered.

A siren screamed inside Cole's head. Amnesia. Concussion. Brain damage. His fault.

Her head jerked upward, and he realized the siren was real, not just inside his own haunted mind.

"Ambulance, police, fire truck…maybe all three," he reassured her. "It's okay." *Liar!*

She nodded. "I know what the sound is. I just don't know who I am."

"Relax. You're probably in shock. You'll be all right in a few minutes." Please, God, she'd be all right in a few minutes. Please, God, he hadn't hurt somebody else. "The blood. Can you tell me where it came from?"

Looking down at her midriff, she brought her hand within half an inch of touching the stain then drew back with a shudder. She bit her lip and shook her head slowly, the slight movement shifting the glow of the streetlights in her shiny hair. "I don't know that either," she whispered.

Maybe she was lying. As a P.I. and a former cop, that should be his first response. They all lied.

But some remnant of the man he once was, some remnant long buried and forgotten, believed she was telling the truth. Her fear was too real.

"Did you have a knife? Did you cut that man who scared you?" he pursued, forcing himself to act on logic, to beat back his unreliable emotions.

"Man?" she repeated blankly.

"You don't remember the man who came up to you, put his hand on your arm, and you started hitting him before you ran into the street?"

She shook her head again. "No. I don't remember

any man.'' Her gaze darted from him to the people, the street, the buildings on one side, the creek on the other. He could see and feel her terror expanding to fill her universe as shock loosened its hold and she realized the extent of what had happened to her. She gripped his arm. ''How did I get here? Where am I?''

A patrol car squealed up with the ambulance right behind. Doors flew open and police and paramedics swarmed out of the two vehicles.

One of the officers was Pete Townley, and Cole was both glad and embarrassed to see his old friend and former partner...and angry at himself for being embarrassed. He had nothing to be ashamed of. He was still performing an honorable service, catching lawbreakers, helping people.

''Hey, buddy,'' Pete greeted him. ''Can't stay away from us, can you? What happened here?''

''This lady ran in front of my car and I hit her.''

Pete turned to his partner, a new guy Cole hadn't met. ''See if you've got any witnesses in the crowd and take their statements. I'll deal with this shady character.'' He grinned.

The team of paramedics rushed over, and for a few moments everything was chaos. The bride with no name clutched Cole's arm convulsively as she shook her head to every request the paramedics made.

''Look, lady,'' one finally exclaimed in frustration. ''We've got certain procedures we have to follow for your benefit and ours. You were hit by a car, and you may have a concussion. Standard procedure is for you to lie on this stretcher, let us fasten this cervical collar on your neck and examine you. Trust me, this won't hurt a bit. You'll feel better and so will we.''

The bride's grip on Cole's arm tightened. ''No.''

Cole patted her hand. "It'll be all right. These men want to help you and I need to talk to the officer a minute."

"Don't leave me! You're the only person I know here." She looked around frantically. "The only person I know in the whole world."

She sure had changed her tune, and it made him damn nervous. Cole had his spot in life. He caught embezzlers, con artists, insurance-scam criminals. What he didn't do—what he hadn't done even when he was on the police force—was successfully rescue damsels in distress.

"You don't know me," he protested.

"Yes," she said, suddenly calmer as she stared directly into his eyes. "Yes, I do know you and I trust you."

He wasn't sure what she saw in his gaze; certainly not the truth or she wouldn't trust him.

"I'm not going anywhere," he said with a sigh. "The cops won't let me leave until they get their pound of flesh."

Reluctantly she consented to lying on the stretcher for the examination, but adamantly refused to permit the paramedics to put on the collar or the backboard. As they checked her vital signs, her gaze remained fixed on him, clutching him as if he were a lifeline. He fought back a laugh...or a grimace...at the irony of that concept.

"Long time no see," Pete said. "What's going on? You so hard up for a woman you've taken to running them down?" Pete grimaced immediately, pulled off his cap and ran a hand through his bright red hair. "Aw, geez, I didn't mean anything by that. I wasn't thinking."

Cole shoved his hands deep into the pockets of his blue jeans and made himself smile. ''Forget it. Hell, I wasn't thinking about Angela either until you started falling all over yourself apologizing.''

It was a lie, but only a half lie. Of course he'd been thinking about Angela, about her still body covered in blood, about her fragility, about his role in her death. Pete's careless joke hadn't affected that one way or the other.

''Listen, you might want to check the sidewalk and the grass for blood or some kind of weapon. She ran from between those buildings and got into a struggle with a sleazy guy who came up, probably harmless, begging, but he did grab her arm. She got away from him and ran into the street, right in front of my car. I don't think she had time to injure the guy, but you never know.''

Pete nodded and went to check out the scene.

Cole could feel the woman's needy eyes on him, pulling him as a magnet, and he returned his attention to her, moving closer to where she lay reluctantly on the stretcher. ''She okay?'' he asked.

''Seems to be,'' one of the paramedics answered. ''We still need to take her in, though. Just a precaution since she appears to have some memory loss.''

''No!'' The bride pushed aside the paramedics and raised herself to a sitting position. Terror showed in her gaze, her trembling lips, the shaky, beseeching hand she lifted to him. ''Don't let them take me. Please don't let him take me!''

He squatted beside her, gently easing her back onto the stretcher. ''Shh. Just relax, okay?''

Him? Don't let him *take me?* Why had she used the singular pronoun the second time when there were two paramedics? Was something else going on here besides a fear of being taken to the hospital by strangers?

"I'm all right now, really I am. I remember my name and where I live. It's…Mary Jackson, and I live at…1492 Main Street."

She was definitely lying now, making it up on the spot, her eyes begging him to believe her, to help her, looking at him as if he were a hero or Marshall Dillon. Well, he wasn't. He was just a former cop who hadn't even been able to protect his own family, so what did she want from him?

He rose abruptly, doing her the favor of breaking away from her.

"What day is it?" the paramedic asked, his voice gentle. He knew she was lying, too.

Tears flooded her eyes, but she bit her lip and blinked them back, then looked around her. The curious crowd chafed at the police tape as they tried to get a closer look, and a steady stream of cars inched along while drivers gawked at the scene.

"Saturday." A good guess from the number of people out and about. "It's Saturday night. I don't know the date. Do you?" she challenged.

Cole shifted his stance from one foot to the other and released a long breath. The woman, in spite of being in a complete panic, not knowing who or where she was, had guts. He had to give her that. "I'll go to the hospital with you," he said, cursing himself even as the words slipped out of his mouth. "I'll follow right behind the ambulance."

She stood and wrapped her arms around herself, then, as if suddenly aware of the bloodstain she was touching, she dropped them to her sides with a shudder. "I can't get in that ambulance. Please don't make me."

Claustrophobia? A bad experience in an ambulance?

"All right, all right," he grumbled. "You can ride with me. I'll take you to the hospital and get you checked in. I guess I owe you that much since I'm the one who ran you down."

But it wasn't only his guilt that motivated him. He wasn't solely responsible for this woman's problems. Something had been wrong with her before she ran in front of his car. A bride in full regalia with blood on her wedding gown had some kind of story to tell, even if she couldn't remember it.

No, it wasn't just the guilt that made him want to take care of her. This woman had that same fragile, helpless, innocent air that Angela had had. And in spite of knowing that the kindest thing he could do was to walk away, he couldn't stop himself from responding to her pleas.

What the hell was the matter with him? Did he have some misguided notion he could get it right this time?

A psychiatrist could probably have a field day with that one.

"Evening, ma'am." Pete strolled up. Cole noted that another squad car had arrived and the officers had taken over the search of the sidewalk and the surrounding area.

Instead of being relieved to see a uniformed police officer, the woman tightened her hold on his arm, and her breathing accelerated.

"Can you tell me what happened?" Pete asked in his best official mode.

"I can't remember," she said, her words barely above a whisper.

"A temporary fugue state," one of the paramedics contributed.

Pete looked at Cole and lifted one eyebrow. "This guy here says you ran out from between those two buildings, a man accosted you and you ran into the street in front of his car. Is that true?"

"I don't know."

"You come from a wedding reception somewhere around here?" Typical cop, assuming she was lying, trying to con her into admitting something. Standard operating procedure, but Cole wanted to tell him to ease up on her, that she was too fragile.

"I told you, I don't remember."

"Where'd you get the blood on your dress?"

"I don't remember!"

"What's your name?"

"I don't remember!"

"She said it was Mary Jackson a few minutes ago," Cole interjected. "Mary Jackson who lives at 1492 Main. But I think she was lying so she wouldn't have to go to the hospital."

Pete's dark eyes bored into her, and she trembled slightly. "Is that your name?" he demanded. "Are you Mary Jackson?"

She looked down to the pavement and shook her head. "I don't know. Maybe. Probably not. Mary Chapin Carpenter sings country music. So does Alan Jackson. I just put them together. 1492 Main Street. *In 1492, Columbus sailed the ocean blue.* And every town has a Main Street. I made it all up. I don't want to go to the hospital."

"Where do you want to go?"

"Home."

"Where might that be?"

Her eyes widened and tears again glistened. "I don't know."

Involuntarily, Cole reached over and squeezed her hand where it clung to his arm. Her skin was smooth and silky, like her dress, and her fingers were long and delicate. The only contrast was a large diamond ring that pressed with sharp cold edges against his fingers.

"The way I see it," Pete continued "you've got two choices, the hospital or the police station. You're going to have some questions to answer when you come out of this *fugue* state, and we need to run some tests on that dress, see what kind of blood that is."

She swallowed, the sound audible over the traffic and crowd noises as if the three of them stood in their own little universe. "What *kind* of blood?"

"Could be human. Or could be chicken. Maybe you were cooking for your own wedding reception. Could be goat. Maybe this was some kind of voodoo ceremony." He stared pointedly at her hand on Cole's arm, at the huge diamond solitaire. "Apparently the wedding wasn't over. You don't have the band to go with that rock."

She held out her hand, studying the ring as if seeing it for the first time. Abruptly she tugged it off and extended it to Cole. "It's not mine!"

"It is unless somebody else claims it," Pete told her. "So what's it gonna be? The station or the hospital?"

Her eyes, the pupils so shrunken they were lost in the silvery-blue mist, silently asked his advice, trusting him to make the right decision, to lead her in the right direction.

Couldn't she tell just by looking at him that the only place he could lead her was straight into hell?

"If I were you, I'd choose the hospital," he growled. "I sure wouldn't voluntarily go with the cops." *And certainly not with an ex-cop who had the scent of death following him like a shadow.*

She studied him a moment longer, her hand still outstretched with the ring winking on her palm. ''All right,'' she said. ''But only if you take me in your car. Only if I don't have to get into that…that thing.''

''I'll take you to the hospital,'' he agreed against his better judgment. She certainly did seem to have a phobia about the ambulance. Of course, she seemed to have a phobia about everything.

Pete cocked an eyebrow at him. ''I don't think that's such a good idea. I think you better let us take care of the lady.''

Cole flinched at his buddy's words. Pete was only following procedure, but it hit Cole hard, like a direct attack, an affirmation that this frightened, confused woman would be better off with anybody in the world except him.

Pete knew his story. So maybe he was saying exactly that.

''Are you arresting me?'' the bride asked, lifting her chin defiantly, that unexpected burst of strength again surfacing.

''No, ma'am. We'd just like to know where that blood came from. I didn't find any more in the vicinity and I didn't find a weapon, but you could have wounded the guy you were struggling with. If you did, he's not around to press charges, and he did accost you first, according to your friend here. We're not arresting you.''

''I'll go to the hospital because I have nowhere else to go, but only if Mr. Grayson takes me.'' She spread her hands several inches away from the dress as if she didn't want to touch it. ''And you're more than welcome to have this...this thing as soon as I get other clothes to wear." She shivered in the warm summer evening. "I don't want it. It makes my skin crawl."

She had amnesia...or a fugue state, as the paramedic called it. She had an aversion to ambulances and hospitals and cops. She was wearing a wedding gown but no wedding band, which probably meant she'd skipped out on her own wedding...after somehow getting blood all over the front of that gown...a gown that made her skin crawl. The only normal things about her were her knowledge of country-music singers and the date America was officially discovered.

She had problems he couldn't even begin to imagine, and she was looking to him to take care of her. What a joke!

"I can get her to the hospital, Pete," Cole snapped. "I can handle that."

"Please take this," she whispered, still holding out her hand.

Pete reached toward her, but she jerked away from him. "I'll take your jewelry in for you, ma'am," he said. "Give you a receipt and you can have it back as soon as you get out of the hospital or anytime you want."

"No. Not you. Him."

"Look, lady," Cole said, "I'm a complete stranger. The only thing you know about me is that I ran you down with my car. Give the ring to the police officer. You give it to me and you may never get it back again. You may never see me again."

"I don't want it back."

"Take it, Grayson," Pete snapped irritably. "We haven't got all night. I'll see that he doesn't run off with it, ma'am."

Cole sighed and reached for the ring, his fingers brushing the smooth coolness of her palm. If he'd had his eyes closed, he'd have been able to tell by the feel that her skin had the color and translucency of fine china, the same allure that invited touching. And the same tendency to shatter.

Get her to the hospital. That was all he had to do. After that, he'd never see her again.

He shoved the gaudy ring into his pocket, turned and strode back to his car. She could follow him or not, go with him or not. He didn't care. He couldn't care.

Chapter Two

Jane Doe.

That's what she'd heard the doctors and nurses calling her when they thought she wasn't listening, and she hated it. Bad enough she'd lost all *memory* of self, but everyone's insistence on using that generic, no-identity name stole any remaining *sense* of self.

They said it was normal that she could remember dates from history and the names of country singers but not whether she liked those country singers, not who she went to concerts with, nothing about the classroom where she'd learned those historical dates. Nothing personal. Nothing that made her anything more than a zombie with no soul and no name.

She tucked the hospital sheet more tightly around her as if that thin material could keep out the demons. She couldn't remember their names or faces, but she knew they were there, watching from dark, soulless eyes, waiting to snare her with twisted claws.

The man who said he'd hit her with his car, Cole Grayson, the one person she'd felt connected to in this strange world, had brought her to the hospital and turned her over to the others then left. They had poked, prodded and examined every inch of her mind and body. She'd hated it, hated the invasion, hated and feared the strangers…medical personnel and police officers…with their questions she couldn't answer and their sly insinuations that she might be lying.

Finally they'd put her in her own room and left her alone, and that was the worst of all. She was alone without even herself for company. But at least she was out of that horrible dress that had imprisoned her with its endless yards of fabric and the sticky blood that stained the front and clung to her skin like some foul creature. Even now, bathed and wearing a clean hospital gown, the metallic scent seemed to linger in her nostrils and on her tongue.

As she lay staring into the darkness, the door to her room opened. It made no sound except for a whisper of a sigh when it moved through the air, but she heard it and a nameless terror rose inside her. Pressing her nails into her palms, she fought the urge to bury her head under the sheet.

Instead, she forced herself to sit up and face the intruder.

He hesitated half in and half out of the doorway, the light from the hall turning him to a dark silhouette, unrecognizable except that he was the only recognizable element in this shadow world she'd been thrust into.

"I thought you'd be asleep," he said. Cole Grayson, the man who'd caused her to be in this hospital in the first place, yet the only person her heart trusted even while her mind warned her against such insanity.

"No. I wasn't asleep."

He moved inside, closed the door and flipped the wall switch, flooding the sterile room with light. He was tall with wide shoulders that stretched the fabric of the blue knit shirt as it molded to clearly defined muscles. Faded jeans hugged muscular thighs. His brown hair was shaggy, had seen too many weeks between haircuts, and his square jaw was accented by the dark shadow of a man who needed to shave twice a day and hadn't.

His appearance said he observed the rudiments of a civilized dress code but actually didn't much care what he looked like. He bordered on disreputable and was surely someone she shouldn't trust at all.

Yet there was a desolate emptiness somewhere behind his brown eyes that reached inside her and drew her to him, a sadness she suspected most people didn't see. It was that desolate emptiness, an echo of what she felt inside herself, that had made her trust him while she was still in the middle of the street, virtually under the wheels of his car.

No, that wasn't all of it. Behind her emptiness lay fear; behind his lay a stone wall strong enough to support that emptiness, to keep it from devouring him. She was drawn to that strength, to that stone wall, to the only security she'd seen so far in this unknown world into which she'd awakened.

"I brought your engagement ring back." He walked over to the bed and laid the shiny object on her nightstand. She looked at it, somehow expecting it to take on a life of its own, to coil and snarl and attack her.

"I must have loved the man who gave it to me," she said quietly.

"Yeah, you must have. I don't think men go around giving that kind of jewelry to women who hate them."

In vain she searched her memory for a picture of that man, for the love she must have felt for him, for some reason that would explain why she had such an aversion to the ring.

"I'm glad you weren't hurt badly," Cole continued. "I talked to the cops, gave them my statement, and the officer said you were okay except for a little bruising, especially around your wrists. That guy you were struggling with must have grabbed you pretty hard."

She lifted her hands and looked at the black-and-blue marks that marred the arms she didn't recognize. Had she always been this thin or had she been sick? What event had occurred in her life to cause that small scar? Did she break that fingernail when she fell or when she grappled with the man on the street...or during whatever struggle had left all that blood on her dress?

"I guess he must have grabbed me hard. I don't remember."

"The doctors think you will, though. Soon."

She nodded. "I know. They told me. Officer Townley said they're checking missing-persons reports and they'll put my picture in the paper and on the news. Somebody will recognize me. The doctor said as soon as I see a familiar face, that could jog my memory." It all sounded quite logical. So why didn't she believe it? Why did she fear being stuck in this foggy land of nowhere for the rest of her life?

"Yeah. The guy who gave you that ring is probably frantic right now. As soon as he sees your picture, he'll come to take you home."

"Yes," she said. "If he's still alive. If he's not the man whose blood was all over my dress." A memory beat leathery bat wings against the dark, closed windows of her mind.

"I don't want that thing," she blurted, scooting as

far away from the diamond and from the almost-memory as she could in the narrow bed.

Cole looked as her as though she were nuts. Well, wasn't she?

He rubbed the back of his neck, the gesture causing his biceps to bulge so that the sleeve of his shirt seemed certain to tear. He was a big man, a strong man. He could hurt anybody he chose to hurt, especially someone as defenseless as she.

Yet she felt no fear of him. Instinctively she knew that he would use that strength to protect her, and she desperately needed protection right now...from the dark, unknown terrors hiding in her mind, as well as from the unknown world around her.

"Who are you?" she asked.

"I told you, I'm Cole Grayson."

"That's not what I mean. They've been calling me Jane Doe. That might even be my name, or maybe it's Sarah Smith or Mary Jackson. But whatever it is, a name doesn't tell anything about who I am or who you are."

He gazed down at her for a long moment then finally turned away and angled a hip onto the windowsill, studying their reflections in the dark glass. "I'm nobody you want to know."

A gray veil of desolation emanated from him. She could see it, feel it in the weight of the air, smell the leaden scent, taste the bitter agony. Perhaps because her mind was completely empty of her own emotions, his came to her, strong and clear.

"I don't have a choice right now," she said. "You're the only person I know."

"What do you know about me, other than the fact that I ran you down in the street?"

"You said I darted in front of your car. If you hadn't acted quickly, I could have been killed. So I guess what I know about you is that you saved my life."

His lips twisted upward in a cynical imitation smile. "That's a nice theory. I'll try real hard to buy into it." His gaze retreated into the shadowed depths of his own soul for a moment, then he shrugged. "Well, I'm glad to see you're doing better."

He was getting ready to leave, taking with him the only connection, tenuous and brief though it was, that she had to herself, to the person she'd been before the accident, the only familiar element in this unfamiliar world.

"Tell me about the man I struggled with," she entreated, interrupting him before he could declare his intention to leave, thereby making it irrevocable. "What did he look like? The police kept asking me, and I don't know. They asked if I knew him, and I don't know. They asked if the blood on my dress belonged to him, if I wounded him, and I don't know." She bit her lip as she realized her voice was rising, panic spilling over the edges of her words.

He moved to sit beside her on the bed, the mattress sinking with his weight, creating the sensation that, if she relaxed, she could slide against his body, into him, let herself be swallowed up in his strength.

She held herself rigidly against the temptation to do just that.

He gazed at her for a long moment and she saw that his eyes were actually hazel, the brown streaked with green like a tree in April, dead from winter's cold but ready to burst into bloom with the warmth of spring. However, the torment that welled up from the depths gave the lie to that green promise.

He raised his hand and for a second she thought he was going to take hers, but instead he raked his fingers through his shaggy hair then dropped them to his denim-encased thigh. "I didn't get much of a look at the guy. Average size, average height, dark hair. I think he was probably a homeless person, looking for a handout. They sleep in the parks around the area. I don't think he meant to hurt you."

"Then I must have had the blood all over me before. Did I? When you first saw me, was there blood on my dress?"

"I don't know." He grinned wryly. "You see? You're not the only one who has to admit that. If you want my opinion, though, I'd say you did. The blood was several minutes old by the time I got to you. That could be one reason that guy approached you. He could have been trying to help a beautiful woman who might be hurt."

An involuntary, unexpected thrill darted through her and she touched her face, examining the unfamiliar contours. "Am I beautiful?"

"You don't know what you look like? No, I guess you don't."

"Nobody had a mirror in the emergency room. They told me to wait until I got up here, but I haven't looked yet. I'm not sure I can deal with seeing a stranger staring back at me." Even as she said it, she felt shame for her cowardice, for being so frightened of everything, even her own face.

"To answer your question, yeah. You're beautiful." His words were complimentary but his tone was cold. For a brief instant, green fire seemed to flicker in the depths of his eyes, a fire that could heat a woman to the boiling point, past that and beyond, a fire that brought her body to tingling awareness. But that green flame died as quickly as it came.

If it had ever truly been there in the first place and not just her imagination, something she wanted to see.

"You're beautiful like one of those cups with flowers painted on them that you see in antique shops," he continued, his words so detached she was sure she'd imagined that brief spurt of flame. "The kind a guy's afraid to pick up because it might break if he held it too tight."

It was a pretty accurate description of the way she felt, but she bristled anyway. "Wouldn't you be feeling a little fragile and a whole lot scared if *you* suddenly lost yourself?" She blurted the defense as much for herself as for him.

"Yeah, I guess I would be." His square, black-stubbled jaw and the straight line of his lips contradicted his words.

With the clarity about others that must have come when she lost herself, she knew that Cole Grayson had met the devil and challenged him on his own turf. Considering the torment that lived behind his eyes, he might have lost the battle, but even so, he'd survived and nothing frightened him anymore.

"Would you hand me that other hospital gown from the foot of the bed?" she asked. "It's the only pretense of a robe they could give me and I want to see what I look like." She wasn't sure whether her sudden courage came from the fact that Cole had enough strength for two people and she was able to absorb some of it, or whether his stoic demeanor shamed her into the action.

He rose from the bed, handed her the gown and waited.

She wrapped it around, covering the open back of the first gown.

Even so, when she stepped out of bed, she felt naked and exposed…and acutely aware of Cole's masculine presence in the small room.

That was silly. The gowns, one tied in the back and the other in the front, hid her body effectively. Anyway, Cole was there as a rescuer. He had certainly not given her any reason to think he was interested in her body. He'd all but said she looked as if she might break if a man held her too tightly…and he looked like a man who would hold a woman very tightly.

She moved around the bed, carefully avoiding the mirror above the sink in the corner of the room. Facing herself wasn't going to be easy.

Cole came up behind her, so close she could feel his body heat, smell his masculine scent combined with something else…something dark and dangerous and scary and exciting.

He flipped on the light above the sink then put both hands on her shoulders. "Go ahead," he urged, his voice as startlingly gentle as his touch. "Maybe when you see yourself, everything will come back. You said the doctors thought the sight of a familiar face might help. You can't get much more familiar than your own."

She lifted her gaze slowly, as if she could sneak up on the strange woman she knew she would find in the mirror.

It was a pale, thin face with prominent cheekbones and overly large eyes. Long blond hair failed to add any color.

The image belonged to her, housed the brain she used to speak and walk. It was the woman other people saw when they looked at her. She ate with that mouth, smelled with that nose, saw through those eyes, combed that hair.

Though she couldn't say the features were familiar, the tight, frightened expression somehow was.

She raised her eyes to Cole's, looking for something—reassurance, courage, answers he couldn't possibly have.

What she found instead was a flaring of the green flame she'd seen so briefly before, a fire that reminded her he was, after all, a man, an attractive, virile man, and she was a woman wearing nothing underneath the short hospital gowns.

For an instant, inappropriate thoughts and feelings flooded her mind and her body. Though Cole didn't move, she could feel his heat against her skin, tracing down her spine and over her bottom, warming her thighs just as his breath warmed the nape of her neck.

He blinked, took his hands from her shoulders and stepped backward. "Recognize anybody?" he asked, his voice gruff with angry overtones. Anger at her? At himself?

"No." Her answer came out on a breathy sigh and she was appalled to find her body yearning for him to return, to stand behind her, to touch her again. Her memory might be gone, but her hormones were working overtime.

Stress, she told herself. *A reaction to the accident, to everything that had happened. So much stress that she'd imagined for a second time the brief flicker of desire in Cole's eyes, imagined it and overreacted.*

She cleared her throat and tried again to answer his question. "If I'd seen a picture, I wouldn't have been able to identify it as me, but I would have known it was familiar.'' At least, the expression was.

''That's a good start.'' He walked away, giving her plenty of space to return to the bed without getting close to him.

She hurried back and pulled the sheet up to her neck. ''Thank you,'' she said. ''For being there just now, I mean. And for saving my life.''

He nodded, compressed his lips and shoved his hands deep into his pockets. ''Well, I just came by to see if there's anything I can do for you, anything you need, other than your memory, of course. I took that away from you, but I'm afraid I can't give it back. No matter what you say, I blame myself that you're here.''

''I don't need anything.'' She tried to sound more certain than she felt. ''I'll probably wake up in the morning with all my memories intact.'' Which didn't mean she wouldn't still be terrified.

''I hope so. I hope that by this time tomorrow you'll be home with the man who gave you that diamond.''

The sparkling ring looked incongruous lying on the nightstand between the plastic tray and plastic water pitcher. She swallowed hard and fought back the resurgence of unreasoning terror and disgust it evoked.

''You need to put it on,'' he said. ''Jewelry has a bad habit of disappearing in hospitals.''

She continued to stare at the ring, unable to force herself to move closer, to reach for it.

Cole picked up the diamond with one hand and took hers with the other.

His hand was warm and big and capable and she fought down a rekindling of that inappropriate response to his touch that she'd felt while standing in front of the mirror. He was being considerate and kind. That was all.

He touched the tip of her finger with the ring, and terror suddenly overwhelmed her again, a black void that drove out any other emotions and threatened to swallow her up, a nameless, pervasive fear that encompassed everything because she couldn't recognize its face.

She bit the inside of her cheek, trying to divert herself, to maintain contact with reality. It was only a ring, not some instrument of torture, nothing to cause her breathing to become labored and her mouth dry.

The metal burned as he slid it onto her finger, then stopped at her second knuckle. "Your finger's swollen, probably from the accident. You'd better wear your ring on a smaller one."

"No!" She snatched her hand away, curling it to her chest and leaving him holding the ring. "It'll fall off," she improvised desperately. "I'll lose it. You take it."

Cole sighed and stepped back. "Lady, do you have any idea how much this ring is worth? Way too much for you to entrust it to a stranger."

"You're no more of a stranger to me than I am to myself. I trust you."

"You don't have any reason to."

"I don't have any reason not to. You asked if there was anything you could do for me. You can take that thing away. Please."

He shook his head then reached inside his pocket and withdrew a battered leather wallet.

"I'll tell you what. I just cashed a check and I've got—" He counted out bills. "Three hundred eighty-five dollars. It's probably not even close to what this rock is worth. But I'll take the ring with me and leave you this so you'll have some money in case your fiancé doesn't show up immediately and so you can have some reassurance that I'll get your diamond back to you.''

''All right.'' She refrained from telling him that she didn't want the money, didn't care if she ever saw the ring again. That would sound crazy.

Besides, she probably would want it back when her fiancé found her, when her memory returned.

Maybe.

Though wanting the vile thing on her finger seemed an impossibility right now.

He gave her the cash then took out a business card and a pen. ''Here's my home and office numbers in case you leave before I get back to you. The home number's unlisted.''

She took the card and read it, memorizing both numbers. Just in case.

He studied the ring again then slid it into his pocket. ''Try to get some sleep, okay?''

She nodded.

''Good night and good luck, uh—''

She held her breath. Was he going to call her *Jane Doe* the way the nurses had, let her know that he didn't consider her a real person either?

''Mary Jackson.'' His lips quirked upward in a semblance of a smile. ''Good thing you're not a rock-music fan. You might have called yourself something really off the wall.''

She tried to return his smile. ''Sure. Things could always be worse. Right?''

He nodded. ''Yeah. Well, I'm sure it'll all work out for you. Good night, Mary. Call me if you need anything.''

He spun on his heel and left, taking his aura of sadness and desolation with him, but instead of feeling lighter, the air seemed heavier and more oppressive than before he'd gone, darker, even though the light still blazed from the ceiling.

Chapter Three

For the next two days and nights Cole saw her haunted, frightened, alluring face on the six o'clock news broadcasts, in the local papers and in his dreams.

Despite all the publicity, however, her groom had not appeared to claim his bride. No one had come in to identify her, to take her home. Every afternoon Cole checked with Pete, and every afternoon the word was the same. Nothing.

She remained a woman with no past, adrift in a world she couldn't remember. And no matter that she genuinely didn't seem to blame him for it...he blamed himself. The accident had been unavoidable, but that didn't change the fact that he'd been the one driving the car, the one who'd caused her problems and, ironically, the only one she'd trusted to help her. He couldn't help her. He knew that.

Yet the memory of the way she'd lifted her chin and lied so bravely about remembering her name and address to keep from going to the hospital, the startled, pleased way she'd looked when he told her she was beautiful...the memory of her...stayed in the forefront of his mind and made him wish he could help her.

Pete had told him that she'd insisted on leaving the

hospital the next day. Using the money he'd loaned her on her engagement ring, she'd rented a hotel room as close as she could get to the scene of the accident, hoping she'd recognize something familiar. He knew the place she'd chosen. It wasn't luxurious nor was it seedy. It was mediocre. Institutional. Not a place where he could imagine Mary, with her air of fragility and dignity, being comfortable.

Cole tried to get the image of her in that hotel out of his mind as he pulled off the street and into his winding, tree-lined driveway a little after midnight. It was a dark, moonless night and, without the reflective strip on his mailbox, he might have missed the turn.

That driveway had been one of the things Angela had liked about the place, that the casual passerby wouldn't be able to find them. On the outskirts of Dallas, the heavily wooded lots were large and had offered the requisite city residence for his job on the police force as well as seclusion and safety for Angela.

Which only proved that nobody could ever really be safe.

Not Angela and Billy in their secluded house and not Mary Jackson in her rented room in a mediocre hotel. But he couldn't do one thing to change that, so why was he even stewing about it?

He pulled into the garage and got out of his car— not the beloved T-bird he'd been driving when he ran into Mary, but a dark blue, midsize sedan, the one he drove when he didn't want to stand out, didn't want to be noticed, when his job called for him to blend into the crowd, as he'd done tonight, infiltrating a society party dressed as a waiter.

He left the garage, closing the door behind him, and crossed his yard. The porch light had burned out a couple of years ago and he'd never replaced it. He liked the darkness.

A cricket chirped, his song loud in the quiet. Something scurried through the underbrush...a raccoon or 'possum, maybe. Too small for a deer. All sorts of wildlife shared the acres of dense woods that surrounded and separated the half-dozen houses in the development.

He strode onto the porch, unlocked the front door and went inside, crossing the entryway and climbing the wide wooden stairs without turning on a light. There was no need. He knew where every piece of furniture was located. He hadn't moved anything in the last three years.

The only thing he'd changed was the room he and Angela had planned to use for a nursery, though the need had never arisen. He'd bought bedroom furniture and that was where he slept. He never entered the room he'd shared with Angela or the one that still held Billy's twin bed surrounded by his stuffed animals and football posters.

The red light on his answering machine blinked in the darkness as he entered. He flipped on the light and pressed the button to retrieve his messages.

"This is...the woman who ran in front of your car two days ago." Her hesitant voice emerged from the plastic machine like a soft spring breeze, and he could almost smell the white flowers with satin petals.

"I thought you might have tried to call me. Someone did—a man, the operator said. But when I answered, no one was there and whoever it was never called back. I thought perhaps it was you since you're the only person besides the police who knows where I am. Although I don't suppose you know, do you? I'm staying in room 428 at the Newton Arms.''

She recited the hotel's number then hesitated as if debating whether to say more. He couldn't tell if she hung up or if her silence triggered the answering machine's automatic disconnect. In any event, the computerized voice announced that the call had come in at 9:23.

Cole played the message again, listening closely to what she *wasn't* saying.

The tight sounds of fear were woven through her precise speech patterns and carefully modulated tones, and every word, every nuance sent guilt shooting through him.

Someone had called her…a wrong number, a reporter, a crank, a nobody…but she was illogically frightened. He'd seen Angela go through that torment a hundred times. Every hang-up call was a potential murderer or kidnapper checking to see if she was home alone.

Not only was he powerless when it came to helping people like Angela and Mary, but he seemed to have a talent for dragging them under, putting them in a position where fears that usually lurked in the background could grab them by the throat.

It was too late to return the call now. Tomorrow morning would have to be soon enough.

He peeled off his clothes and tossed all of them, even the uncomfortable, rented waiter's uniform, into a pile in one corner then went down the hall to shower.

The cool water felt good sluicing down his body, washing off the stench of cigarette smoke, alcohol and cloying perfume.

Tonight he'd served drinks and hors d'oeuvres at the

party while observing and surreptitiously taking pictures of a woman wearing the jewelry she'd reported to her insurance company as stolen. He'd been successful. His employer would be pleased.

But he didn't feel successful. He felt useless, unfocused, as though he was just stumbling along down the road of life with no purpose and no goal.

Actually, that wasn't completely true. His mind had consistently focused on one thing tonight…the wrong thing. Tonight's job—like many of his assignments—was a no-brainer. He'd had nothing to distract him from thoughts of Mary Jackson.

As he'd offered fresh drinks, taken away dirty glasses and emptied ashtrays, her face had kept intruding, a small, pale image that loomed larger and larger, her eyes begging him for help he couldn't give no matter how much he wanted to.

Then someone would speak to him or bump into him and he'd realize he'd been thinking only of Mary, had lost even the little attention he needed to perform his job. When that happened, he'd forcibly banish her from his thoughts, at least for a few minutes.

Now, after hearing her voice again, he found he couldn't get her out of his head even for a few minutes. And it was more than guilt, more than a futile desire to help her and salve his conscience.

He couldn't stop thinking about her smooth, porcelain skin…her long, graceful legs when she'd slid out of bed wearing that short hospital gown…the scents of harsh hospital soap that almost but not quite overpowered her white floral fragrance…the hungry way his body had responded to her nearness…and the brief flash of desire he'd seen in her eyes when they'd met his in the mirror.

He twisted the faucets angrily, shutting off the flow of water the way he wished he could shut off such troublesome thoughts, then, with a muttered curse, dried his body that had responded much too eagerly just to the thought of her.

He returned to his bedroom, flopped onto the unmade bed and switched out the light.

Okay, she was a woman, he was a man, and he lusted for her. So?

So that didn't make any sense. He knew better than to lust after women with haunted, frightened eyes who needed a champion, a knight in shining armor. He lusted after women with knowing eyes, strong women who needed only what he had to give. And lust was all he had to give.

In spite of the fact that he was exhausted, sleep was elusive. When it finally came, he slept hard and long, waking shortly after nine.

Immediately, even before he made coffee, he called the Newton Arms, but Mary Jackson had already checked out.

He tried to call Pete, at home first since it was Saturday, but got the answering machine. He wasn't at work, either, so Cole left a message at both places then went downstairs, made a pot of coffee, drank it and had ample time to wonder why he wasn't pleased that someone—her fiancé?—must have come to claim Mary.

Because he sensed that her fears were of much longer standing than the normal disorientation that amnesia would cause anyone? Because the situation brought back the awful sense of helplessness he'd gone through with Angela?

Because the additional element of sexual attraction

had, against all reason and common sense, insinuated itself into the equation?

When the phone finally rang, he snatched it up, half expecting, half hoping it would be her calling to tell him where she was.

"What's up, buddy?" Pete asked.

Cole was both disappointed and relieved. "The woman I hit—"

"Mary," Pete interjected. "She asked us to call her Mary Jackson. Sounds better than Jane Doe since that's what we call all the unidentified female bodies that come through here."

Cole flinched at the image of Mary on a slab in the morgue. She'd come awfully close to that. If he'd been going a little faster—

"I've still got her ring, you know, and when I called her hotel, she'd checked out."

"Yeah, I just got back from taking her to the Gramercy shelter for a few days. She freaked this morning when I called to tell her that we got the lab results back, and the blood on her dress is definitely human. She started babbling about how she had to get out of that hotel because *he* knew she was there. Of course, when I asked who *he* was, she didn't know and admitted she wasn't being logical. Seems somebody called her and hung up and she's positive it wasn't a wrong number or a bad connection. Pretty paranoid, but maybe that comes with the amnesia."

"No accident victims in the local hospitals that might belong to that blood?"

"None that admit it. I told her if we got any unidentified bodies, we'd like her to come down and take a look."

"I'm sure that thrilled her."

"About as much as when I told her about Sam Maynard coming in yesterday and trying to claim her—"

"Sam the Sleaze?" Cole flinched at the thought of the disgusting pervert coming into contact with Mary's confusion and vulnerability. "Is he out of jail again? When are you going to put that creep away for good?"

"When he does something we can get him on. He's a sicko, but he's smart enough to ride the line between annoying women enough to get his wrists slapped and annoying them enough to get himself a prison term."

"You think he'd go after her? You think he called her?"

"Sam? Nah. That's not his style. Too much trouble. He can find plenty of women to accost right on the city streets."

"If he was hanging around the station, he might have heard somebody mention where she was staying."

"Could be, but I doubt it. Anyway, when Sam reaches out to touch somebody, he likes it to be in person."

"Pete, you're about as funny as a bad case of the flu."

"I'll tell you what's funny, this whole case. I thought it would be open and shut. If you got a bride, the groom can't be far behind, right? Whole thing's damn odd."

"Yeah, it is. Well, I'm glad you got her installed at Gramercy. She ought to feel safe there."

Cole knew the small shelter Pete was talking about. Next door to a church and staffed by the members, it catered to families and people temporarily down on their luck. A good choice, as shelters went. Nevertheless he had a hard time picturing her there. "I'm going to see her, take her ring back. I'll reassure her that Sam's harmless.''

''Good deal. We're doing what we can on this end, but with no evidence that a crime's been committed, we can't dedicate a lot of manpower to it. Well, I got another call. Check you later, buddy.''

After talking to Pete, Cole went into the small room downstairs that he used for a home office. Other than sleeping in his bedroom and storing beer in the kitchen, this was the only room in the house that he used. He had an official office in a nearby business area, a place to meet clients, but this was where he kept his files and did most of his work. This was the room that justified his holding on to a house he didn't like or want, a house that reminded him every day of his failure.

He opened the top drawer of the desk and took Mary's ring from its hiding place at the back. In the palm of his hand, the gold shone and the diamond sparkled. It was a beautiful ring, and Mary hated it.

Kind of like the way he felt about this house.

In his own way, he was as helpless as she. He couldn't rescue her, couldn't locate her relatives or bring back her memory or even save her from her own fears. Any gallant impulses he had in that direction were pointless.

But he did know someone who would give her a fair appraisal of the ring and loan her money on it. He could contribute that much to easing the trauma of the situation he'd put her in, that much and nothing more.

No matter how much his libido might want him to get more involved.

MARY SAT on the curb in front of the Gramercy Home and tried to push down the panic that threatened to overwhelm her. She had to think, to figure out what to do next, and next after that, what to do with the rest of her life in case nobody showed up to tell her who she was, in case she never remembered.

The church that sponsored the shelter owned the entire block as well as the parsonage across the street. The surrounding neighborhood was quiet, an area of older homes, some well kept, some neglected. Overhead, the sun shone cheerfully from a cloudless blue sky and the smell of honeysuckle was sweet on the summer air. She could not have been in less threatening surroundings. Yet the nameless, faceless fear she'd known since the accident refused to leave her.

In her small hotel room on the fourth floor of the Newton Arms, she'd felt isolated, trapped and claustrophobic yet unable to force herself to venture outside. Though she'd let the doctor at the hospital convince her to find a room close to the place where she'd appeared in the hope that familiar surroundings would bring back memories, she was terrified of the area, terrified to leave the hotel.

The hang-up phone call she'd received last night had increased her anxiety. Moving to another area of town, to this shelter recommended by Officer Townley, should have solved those problems. But it hadn't. Now she felt exposed and vulnerable.

It had nothing to do with the dozen or so other inhabitants of the small shelter. They were basically in the same circumstances as she…homeless, unemployed, no friends or loved ones to care for them. Though actually they were better off than she was. They had memories of homes and loved ones. They knew their own names.

Nor was her feeling of vulnerability directly related

to Sam Maynard, the strange man whom Officer Townley said had claimed to be her fiancé. True, the panic had wrapped around her with suffocating intensity at that news and hadn't completely dissipated with Townley's assurances that the man was essentially harmless and had no way of knowing where she was staying. The hang-up call the previous evening could have been from him.

But her fear went beyond such specifics. It was free-floating, attached to nothing and everything, all-consuming and illogical.

After completely breaking down that morning when Officer Townley had hit her with the double blow of the pervert who'd wanted to take her home and then told her the blood on her dress was human, she'd resolved to take control, to refuse her fear the power it demanded. Even if she never regained her memory, if no one ever came to take her back to her home and family, she would conquer this unreasoning terror.

A nondescript dark blue sedan pulled over to the curb and her determination vanished as a black dread encompassed her. Her heart began to pound irregularly, perspiration beaded on her forehead and the muscles in her stomach knotted almost painfully. As she got to her feet, her movements seemed to be the slow motion of a nightmare.

Someone coming to the church, she told herself. *Someone coming to offer a job to one of the people in the shelter. Someone harmless!*

She clenched her fists even as her body involuntarily turned to run back to the shelter.

"Mary!"

She choked down a sob as she recognized the voice,

one of the few she could recognize, the only one that didn't frighten her. Cole Grayson.

He got out of the car and came around to where she stood. Both his blue jeans and the beer logo on his T-shirt were faded and comfortable-looking. He'd shaved but his hair was still shaggy. The sight of him was marvelously, wondrously familiar.

He smiled and the corners of his eyes crinkled in a sunburst pattern, a reflection of the sunburst that had spread through her breast at his appearance.

"You sure look different in those jeans than you did in that wedding dress," he said.

The mention of the dress dimmed that sunburst and shot a painful spasm of unfocused dread through her.

His smile changed to a scowl. "Are you okay? You look like you're about to pass out or something." He took her arm, supporting her. The dependency she felt on him, the reassurance and comfort his touch brought her were totally at odds with her resolution to be strong and conquer her fears.

"I'm fine."

Concern blended with the desolation in his gaze and told her that he knew she was lying, and she hated that.

She didn't want anyone's concern or pity.

Especially not Cole Grayson's.

With a sinking feeling, she admitted to herself that this need came from more than her pride. She wanted this man to view her as a woman, not a victim. She wanted to see that momentary flare in his eyes that she'd seen or imagined when he'd stood behind her at the mirror in the hospital.

"I got your message last night," he said, "but it was too late to call."

"That's okay." Even as she'd dialed his number,

she'd known deep inside that he hadn't been her hang-up caller, and she wasn't sure why she'd called him. It had taken seeing him in person, feeling his hand on her bare arm, for her to realize why. She'd wanted an excuse to talk to him, to see him again, to feel his touch.

She turned and walked a few feet away, removing her arm from his hand, her body from the vicinity of his, even though such action didn't remove the growing attraction she felt for him.

He didn't follow but stood watching her, squinting into the sun. "It was probably a reporter trying to get an interview."

"Why would a reporter hang up?"

"I don't know. Lost his nerve. Got another call. Could be anything."

"How could he find me? The police said they wouldn't tell anybody where I was staying."

He gave an unamused bark of laughter. "Pete—Officer Townley wouldn't. But there are some others who would. Don't underestimate the power of the media. Anyway, maybe it wasn't a reporter. Maybe it was a wrong number."

She shook her head. "I asked the operator. She said the person asked for Mary Jackson."

"Then it had to be somebody who got their info from the cops. Heck, it could have been one of the officers calling to check on you, and he got another call just before you answered. It happens all the time."

"There was a man who came to the police station claiming to be my fiancé."

Cole's lips thinned and his eyebrows drew together in an expression of anger. "Sam Maynard. Pete told me. Yeah, it could have been Sam calling, though that's not what he usually does. Anyway, he's harmless.''

He's harmless! He's harmless! The words reverberated round and round in the empty caverns once occupied by memories of her life, bringing a wintry chill incongruous with the summer day.

''No, he's not.'' The sound of a woman's voice startled Mary, and she almost looked around for the stranger until she realized it was she who had spoken the words. She wasn't sure where they'd come from or who *he* was or why she knew he wasn't harmless.

Cole's eyebrows drew even closer together and he studied her intently. ''I guess it depends on how you define *harmless*,'' he admitted, obviously assuming she'd been talking about Sam Maynard. ''Sam likes to touch women, their hands, their hair, their shoulders…or whatever he can reach. He's a sleazy pervert. I just meant he's never physically harmed anybody. He doesn't go out of his way to pursue his victims, either, so I don't think you have anything to worry about from him.''

He was being logical and making perfect sense, but none of it in any way lightened the terrible sense of dread that phone call had left her with.

She nodded, knowing she had no legitimate reason to disagree with him and trying to make herself believe he was right.

''Can we go inside?'' he asked. ''Somewhere private? We need to talk about this diamond ring of yours.''

Her mouth went dry at the mention of the object.

He lifted his hands as if to ward off what he knew she was going to say. ''I understand that you don't want it back right now, but I don't feel good about keeping it. I can take you to a guy I know who deals in jewelry and precious metals. Kind of an upscale pawnshop. He'll lend you some money, probably one heck of a lot more than what I gave you.''

She looked back toward the shelter, reluctant to have him see her in such needy circumstances, to reinforce his concern and sympathy. ''There's nowhere private in there. One woman has a baby who cries a lot and someone else has a couple of young kids. Even the sleeping cubicles are open.'' And she had no idea how she was going to sleep at night, exposed and vulnerable like that.

He jammed his hands into his pockets and uttered a soft oath.

''It's not so bad,'' she said hastily, contradicting her own thoughts. ''And I won't be here long. I'm going to see about getting a job at a fast-food place. I can't just sit around while I'm waiting to remember who I am.'' She had tossed out the plan without thinking, merely something to reassure Cole that she was all right, that she didn't need his pity, but as she spoke, she knew that was exactly what she wanted to do…get a job, focus on something other than her problems. Then maybe she could forget to be afraid.

''How? You don't know your social security number.''

Her resolve wilted. Beaten before she even got started. With a sigh she walked over to the curb and sat down again, resting her chin in her hands and trying hard not to give in to tears.

She felt him come up behind her, felt his approach in the warm tingles up and down her spine, in his wonderfully familiar scent that both attracted and frightened her.

He sat beside her. "Look, I know some people and can probably pull a few strings to get you a temporary job. That's all you need, anyway…something to fill your time until your fiancé gets here."

Another chill zigzagged through her, and she shivered in the heat. "If he's alive," she whispered. "Officer Townley said the blood on my dress was human."

"Which doesn't mean your fiancé's dead. If they'd found any unclaimed bodies with that type blood, they'd damn sure have pulled you in for questioning."

"They're checking with the hospitals and the morgue today and they'll want me to come down and look at…at anyone they find. Officer Townley said they don't think the blood belongs to the man you saw me struggling with because there aren't any other signs around." She picked up a small pebble from the street and bounced it in one hand. "Maybe that's why I can't remember. Maybe it wasn't the trauma of being hit by a car but the trauma of killing somebody. Somebody I know. Knew."

"Killing somebody?" He caught her hand in a firm clasp. She let the pebble fall to the street and lifted her face to his. In the bright light, his eyes were more green than brown, searing every inch of her face as they flicked over it, bringing the blood rushing to the surface and more than replacing the heat that chill had stolen. "You didn't kill anybody," he said.

She swallowed hard and licked her dry lips as she tried to find her voice, to ignore the sensation of his fingers wrapped around hers, his thigh pressed against hers, the scent of danger that lingered about him and blended with the exhilarating, turbulent way his touch made her feel. "You don't know that."

"No, I don't, but I'd be willing to bet money on it."

"Why?"

"Gut feeling. It's never wrong, and it's saved my life more than once."

"Saved your life?" She pulled away from him and stood, trying to regain her senses. "You never did tell me who you are, what you do."

He rose also and shrugged, looking down the street rather than at her. "I'm a private investigator. I find missing people who don't want to be found, infiltrate big companies and risk terminal boredom to track down embezzlers, crash private parties to save insurance companies from paying false claims. Do you want to go with me to see my friend about the ring? It's just a few miles from here. Have you had lunch yet? We could grab some while we're out."

She had a gut feeling, too, and that gut feeling told her that Cole Grayson had a lot of secrets…those that had caused the barren desert in his gaze and those that caused the aura of danger surrounding him. He hadn't lied to her, but he hadn't told her the entire truth, either. She did know one truth about him, though. He was not a man that the faint-of-heart could exist alongside.

And she certainly fell into the faint-of-heart category.

But she wasn't going to stay that way.

"Yes," she said, lifting her head and forcing the word. "I want to go to see your friend. And no, I haven't eaten."

"Great." Cole strode over to the blue sedan and opened the door for her.

"This isn't the same car you were in the other night," she said.

"No, it's not. This is my work car." He shrugged.

"And it's got air-conditioning. I thought you might be more comfortable."

His work car. The other car had been a restored Thunderbird, obviously a treasure. This car was nothing personal to him. Inviting her into this car was simply giving her a ride, an act of kindness. He wasn't giving anything of himself. And that, she thought, was the essence of Cole Grayson.

She slid inside and Cole started to close the door, when one of the volunteers from the shelter came running out.

"Ms. Jackson! There's a police officer on the phone who wants to talk to you."

The terror again swept over her, swirling through her like a black, destructive tornado. Had someone from her past finally found her? Had Sam Maynard done something else? Had the police found a body?

Why did all those prospects terrify her equally? Shouldn't the thought of recovering her past make her happy instead of frightened?

"I'll go in with you," Cole offered.

"No." She desperately wanted and needed him to come with her. Therefore, she couldn't let him. Somewhere along the line, she was going to have to learn to stand on her own.

"Yes," he countered, and she didn't have the strength to protest a second time.

As she made her way back inside the shelter, through the noisy main room and into a private office, she could feel Cole's presence behind her, supporting her and giving her strength as surely as if he were physically touching her.

She picked up the telephone on the desk. "Hello?"

"This is Pete Townley. We've got a John Doe down

here we'd like you to come look at. Fished him out of the river this morning. He's been dead about two days, has type AB blood, the same as what was on your dress, and multiple stab wounds.''

Stab wounds.

The cold, shiny blade of a knife slashed through her mind.

A torrent of red burst over her, filling her nostrils with a coppery scent and her soul with unbearable horror.

She had to get away from it, run as fast and as far as she could, into the dark oblivion that beckoned her with its promise of escape.

''Mary?'' Strong arms gripped her, pulling her back from the edge. ''Mary!''

She clutched Cole's chest like a lifeline, holding herself barely out of the void.

That must be what had happened before. She'd allowed herself to seek the relief of complete forgetfulness when her life became unbearable.

Had she just retrieved the first memory of that life? If so, she didn't want it!

''There was so much blood,'' she whispered.

''Whose blood?''

The prosaic question snapped her completely back to the present. She looked into Cole's dark eyes, now shadowed with concern. He'd been able to pull her back because he'd known where she was going. He'd been there himself.

Whatever had happened, whatever she'd done, she had to face it the way he'd faced his nightmare.

She realized she still clutched the telephone receiver in one hand while a small voice asked, ''Are you there? Mary? Hello?''

With a strength she hadn't known she possessed, she pushed away from Cole, into the thin air of the world, and lifted the receiver to her ear. "I'll be there to look at the body," she said, forcing the words up her constricted throat and past her dry lips.

Chapter Four

Cole had been present many times when someone had to look at a body. Most of them cried, especially the women and some of the men…cried from grief if they knew the person, from relief if they didn't. Some of them passed out. Some got sick.

Mary just stood beside the slab in the morgue, trembling, arms wrapped around herself, staring down at the body.

"Look familiar?" Pete asked. "Ring any bells? Set off any alarms?"

She shook her head, the movement jerky.

In spite of knowing he couldn't help her and should stay as far away as possible so he didn't make matters any worse, Cole wrapped a comforting arm around her and pulled her rigid body against him.

"Nobody you know? You're sure?" Pete pursued, and Cole resisted the urge to tell him to back off. Pete was only doing his job, the same job Cole himself had done many times. It couldn't be helped that Mary wasn't strong enough for this kind of ordeal. Some people just weren't, and there was nothing he or Pete or anyone else could do to change that.

"How can I tell if it's somebody I know when I

didn't recognize my own face two days ago?'' she whispered.

"Let's go," Cole said, gently turning her away from the cold marble slab with its grisly occupant. "She can't tell you anything, Pete."

Pete nodded. "Thanks for coming down."

When they finally got back outside the building, into daylight and warmth, Mary stopped on the sidewalk and drew in a deep breath.

"I never thought I'd enjoy the smell of exhaust fumes," she said in a shaky voice.

"Yeah, I guess it does beat the hell out of smelling death and decay." He had to admit, he shared her relief at getting out of the morgue. The place had been a part of his life for twelve years and he'd thought himself immune to its horrors, but today Mary's distress had affected him, had made its way inside his pores.

Empathy.

Guilt.

"I need to get used to that, don't I?" she said, staring across the street toward the parking lot but, he suspected, not really seeing it. She held her hands at her sides, clenched into tight fists.

"Probably. Every stiff they dig up that has AB blood, they're going to want you to come take a look. It could be worse. Could have been type O blood on that gown. A more common blood type, more bodies."

She grimaced. "Yes, I suppose things could always be worse."

She didn't sound as if she believed her own statement, and he didn't blame her. Things were pretty bad in her life right now.

"You ready to go get some lunch and visit with my friend about the ring?" he asked, thinking how small a contribution he was offering to her well-being, considering the major contribution he'd made to her problems.

"I'm not hungry. I think I'd like to go straight back to the shelter."

"You're so thin. You need to eat." He wanted to bite back the words as soon as he said them. He sounded like her father, for crying out loud. She was a grown woman, capable of making her own decisions. She didn't need anybody to take care of her.

She's a frightened, vulnerable woman alone without even her memories. And no matter what anybody said, he'd had a hand in making her that way. He had a responsibility even though he wasn't sure he could fulfill that responsibility.

"They'll have lunch at the shelter. I really need some time to deal with this."

She was going to deal with it on her own. He was off the hook.

But something deep inside didn't quite buy it as he thought of her in that crowded, anonymous shelter, eating anonymous food among strangers, sleeping with no privacy. She wasn't strong, couldn't stand alone. If he hadn't run into her, she'd be safe in a comfortable home somewhere with a fiancé who loved her and could take care of her instead of planning to return to that place for people who'd lost their lives.

Nevertheless, he didn't know what he could do to help at this point.

"I understand," he forced himself to say. "We'll visit my friend tomorrow." With one hand he gestured to his car in the parking lot across the street, resisting the urge to place that hand at her waist, guide her, touch her. Any excuse to touch her. He sensed she felt the same attraction he did, but he wasn't going to start down that road, take advantage of her helpless, needy situation.

Especially not with her engagement ring burning a hole in his pocket and the man who gave it to her probably frantic with worry by now.

As she started to step off the curb, a delivery van zipped past, pulled over and parked a few yards up the street…and Mary whirled around, eyes wide, pupils shrunken to pinpoints, face ghostly pale, sheer panic in total possession of her.

He grabbed her as she lunged forward in an effort to run down the walk, get away from the harmless van.

"It's okay! It's okay!" He held her tightly as she struggled to get free. Over and over he repeated the nonsensical phrase. Of course it wasn't *okay* when any-body was that terrified. He'd said the same thing over and over for Angela and achieved only minimal, tem-porary results, never anything approaching *okay*.

Gradually she stopped fighting him, closed her eyes and slumped in his arms. For a moment he thought she might have fainted.

She drew in a deep breath and her spine stiffened, though she kept her face turned to his shoulder. "I'm sorry." Her voice was soft with a slight quaver but an underlying determination. "I have no idea what just happened."

"The van," he speculated. "It's basically the same kind of vehicle as the ambulance you didn't want to get into the other night. You must have some kind of phobia about ambulances."

Maybe she wasn't completely off base about the blood belonging to her fiancé. Maybe she had a phobia about ambulances because he'd been taken away in one, though Cole certainly didn't think she'd put him there.

He could be wrong, of course. She could have been a completely different person before her memory loss. But he didn't think so. Her kind of helpless terror was bone-deep and came from the soul.

She nodded, still not looking at him, as if she was embarrassed over her outburst. "It's hard to fight your fears when you don't know what causes them."

She sounded quite rational. She'd be fine. He should release her, let her stand without his support, take her back to the shelter and leave her alone to cope with things as best she could.

He *should* release her, but, damn, she felt good in his arms. Now that her panic had subsided, she was no longer a victim but merely a beautiful woman...a woman with rounded breasts beneath her white cotton blouse, breasts that were pressed against him because he held her so tightly, one hand at her slim waist and the other splayed across her back. Her hair the color of moonlight was long and soft and brushed his hand as she leaned her head back to look up at him. Her full lips were slightly parted as if she knew he wanted to kiss them...as if she wanted him to kiss them.

Desire and guilt and some crazy need to atone for the past by taking care of her mingled and swirled through his brain, taking control of his mouth and vocal cords.

"Come home with me."

Again her eyes widened, but this time the pupils were dilated.

He did release her then, and she stepped back.

"I didn't mean that the way it sounded." *The hell he didn't!* "Look, it's my fault you have amnesia."

"No," she denied, shaking her head slowly. "I don't think the accident caused it. Even if it did, I ran in front of your car."

"Say what you want, but I feel responsible. I don't want you to go back to that shelter. I have a huge house with two unused bedrooms. You can talk to Pete. He's known me for years. He'll vouch for me. All I'm offering is a place for you to stay until you find out where you belong. I work long hours. I won't be around to bother you, and the cleaning lady just came, so she's not due back for another couple of weeks. You'll have the place to yourself most of the time."

Oh, Lord, what was he saying? Why couldn't he stop the flow of insanity? He was way beyond asking her to stay with him because he wanted to protect her. He simply wanted her with him. He simply wanted her.

"My place has a state-of-the-art burglar alarm system," he continued, making himself focus on the important part of his offer, the only part he could deal with, her safety. "It's in the city, so help is ten minutes away, but it's surrounded by an acre of trees. You can't even see my closest neighbors. You'll feel safe there."

She licked her lips and looked at the innocuous delivery van that had sent her into such a panic.

"All right," she said, and when she turned back to him, he saw the first flicker of hope in her eyes.

That flicker almost undid him, almost made him withdraw the offer.

But maybe she would feel safe in his home. Maybe she would *be* safe at least for a few days, until she could return to her own home.

"Don't you want to call Pete and check me out first?"

She frowned. "No. I trust you more than I trust him. Why should I call him?"

He wanted to tell her not to trust him, not to count on him because he couldn't deliver. All he was offering her was a physical shelter and that wouldn't be enough to protect her from the horrors that lived inside her own mind.

MARY KNEW she ought to feel apprehensive about her decision to stay with a man who was, like everybody else, a total stranger. However, as they drove through the streets of a city she should recognize but didn't, she felt a vast sense of relief.

In the seat beside her, Cole loomed as a solid, dependable presence. He slouched comfortably, guiding the car with the fingers of one hand at the bottom of the steering wheel, in control without making an effort.

His profile as he stared out the windshield appeared to be chiseled from sun-browned granite. When he spoke, pointing out landmarks in an effort to jog her memory, she was always a little surprised at the supple movements of the mouth and jaw that appeared so rigid otherwise.

She'd had to stop herself more than once from wondering how those lips would feel on hers, if they'd be soft with a hint of underlying rigidity, warm like the afternoon sun that slanted through the windshield and caressed the skin on her arms. For a few moments as they'd stood on the sidewalk outside the morgue, she'd thought he was considering kissing her. If he felt any of the same compelling attraction she felt, going home with him might not be a wise thing to do.

That was the only apprehension she felt about staying with Cole Grayson, the impossible feelings that went one step beyond a dependency on his strength, the attraction that made her want more from him than protection and strength.

The sound of the car's turn signal interrupted her thoughts, and she looked up to see a large grocery store in front of them.

"I thought I'd pick up a few things." Cole parked then looked at her with one of his rare smiles. "Unless you want sardines in mustard sauce with a cold beer for dinner tonight and again for breakfast in the morning."

Mary returned his smile. "For all I know, that could be my normal diet. But I have to admit, it doesn't sound very appealing."

Inside the store she was surprised to find that, while she couldn't specifically remember eating certain foods, she did have definite ideas of what she liked and didn't like. "No liver," she said, shuddering as she stared down at the dark meat.

Cole chuckled. "Smart lady. We'll get some steaks and chicken. How about broccoli?"

"Only with cheese sauce."

As they went through the store, discussing and selecting items of food, Mary found herself relaxing, the ever-present fear dissipating into the mundane shelves of food. She felt almost as if she had a life, as if she and Cole were friends...or something more than friends...who shared a past and shopped for groceries together on Saturday afternoons. It was all a lie; she knew that. But the respite from emptiness and fear was a welcome one.

Cole's home was only a few minutes from the store and Mary's comfort level rose another notch as they turned off the street onto an almost invisible driveway then traveled a short distance through thick, concealing woods. The house was two-story, built from native stone that blended into the woodsy setting. Like Cole, his home seemed a sturdy, impenetrable fortress, hidden from the world.

Holding the bag of groceries in one hand, he unlocked the front door with the other and moved back for her to precede him.. As she stepped onto the solid marble of the entryway and looked into the spacious living room, for the first time in her limited memory, she felt safe from the nameless terrors that stalked her.

A large picture window took up most of one wall, but even though the drapes were open, the trees outside were so thick and so close that she didn't feel exposed. A long navy-blue sofa faced the tall stone fireplace and dominated the room. A matching oversize recliner and irregularly shaped coffee table, its top carved from some dark, shiny wood at least a couple of inches thick, added to the feel of solidity. Every surface was spotless, and vacuum cleaner tracks crossed the plush tan carpet. Mary recalled that Cole had said the cleaning lady had just been there, which explained the immaculate condition, but even so, the comfortable, inviting room seemed somehow desolate and abandoned, not lived-in.

"You have a lovely home," she said.

"Thanks." He stood just inside the door, clutching the bag of groceries, his expression tight as he stared at the wide staircase opposite the living room.

What, she wondered, had caused his sudden mood change? Was he regretting his offer for her to stay there? Or was she imagining the mood change? "The bedrooms are upstairs," he said. "In case you want to get settled in. Put your things away."

"Yes, I'd like that." Though she carried in one shopping bag the few clothes and toiletries she'd purchased, it would feel good to put them out somewhere, to have one small area where she belonged, even if only temporarily. "Which room should I use?"

She hadn't imagined his change of mood. A battle raged across the angles of his face, in his dark eyes, in the tight lines around his mouth and the tortured set of his jaw. He drew in a long, hard breath then let it out on a casual shrug, the gesture belying the anguish she'd just witnessed. "Your choice," he said, his voice noncommittal and empty. "It doesn't matter. Let me put these groceries in the kitchen and I'll go up with you."

He turned and walked away.

Mary waited, studying the two closed doors at the top of the stairs with trepidation. The light mood she'd found in the grocery store and on the drive here had vanished with Cole's. What was up there that caused Cole so much distress? What could possibly await her behind the closed doors of the bedrooms?

Cole returned from the kitchen, his expression grim as he came up beside her then paused for a moment before starting up the stairs.

Mary followed, her footsteps dragging.

On the landing he stopped in front of the door on the left and closed the fingers of one hand around the metal knob. "This room will probably be more comfortable," he said, looking down at his hand that held but didn't turn the knob. "It's the master bedroom. I haven't been in either of these rooms for three years, but Ethel cleans them regularly. Angela and Billy, my wife and stepson, have been dead for three years. "

Angela and Billy, my wife and stepson? Dead for three years?

Slowly he turned the knob, and suddenly her heart-beat went into double time. The nameless, irrational fear hit again, and she felt that if she went into that room, she might never come out again.

As he opened the door and stepped aside for her to enter, for an instant her vision blurred and she saw a dim room with dark, heavy furniture. For that instant, terror rose in her throat and stole her breath and she thought she would suffocate, but then the vision disappeared, sucked back into the black void of her mind.

In its place was a light, spacious room. Dust motes danced in the late-afternoon sun as it filtered through lace curtains and dappled the polished wood of an ornate dresser. A spread of pale blue with white swirls covered the king-size bed and was complemented by a lacy dust ruffle and pillow shams.

Unlike the living area downstairs, a woman had obviously occupied this room. The dresser held an assortment of feminine paraphernalia—a tall wooden jewelry box with etched glass doors through which she could see flashes of gold, a mirrored tray holding several bottles of perfume and a couple of lipsticks, and a porcelain ring holder with two rings. A picture sat on top of the chest of drawers in the opposite corner. In the studio portrait, Cole stood with one arm around a small, dark-haired woman and the other resting on the shoulder of the boy in front of them.

She shook her head and backed from the room. "I, uh, could I see the other room, please?" Even as the words left her mouth, Mary knew she sounded ungrateful, but she also knew she could never sleep in the sunny, happy room where Cole and Angela had slept as husband and wife.

"I understand," he said, his voice and face devoid of expression as he closed the door behind her.

Mary refrained from asking him to explain it to her since she didn't understand her aversion to the room at all. She barely knew Cole. His relationship with another woman, his deceased wife, couldn't—shouldn't—bother her.

He strode across the hall and opened the door on the opposite side. "This was Billy's room."

Posters of Cowboys football players hung on the walls, and the twin bed was topped by a spread featuring footballs, gold and silver helmets and lots of Cowboys banners. Stuffed animals perched in orderly rows on shelves. A baseball, bat and glove occupied one corner. A computer sat on a child-size desk. This room, like the other, had the appearance of an inhabitant who would return at any minute.

Mary swallowed hard, pushing down the sensation of overpowering loneliness and sorrow that the room evoked as it sat waiting for the little boy who would never return.

"Thank you," she said. "This will be fine." Perhaps she should have stayed at the shelter.

But she couldn't have done that. However out of place she might feel invading Cole's secret places, the bond she felt with him was so strong, she could never have refused his offer, the chance to be near him.

"Good. There are still things in the drawers and closets, but you can move them or push them aside, whatever you need to do," Cole said. She watched his throat move as he, too, swallowed, probably pushing down the same sensations of loneliness and sorrow as she had only moments before. "I'll go put on the steaks while you settle in."

He left, and Mary entered Billy's room, feeling like an intruder as she set her shopping bag on the floor. She wouldn't take out anything and create her own space after all. The drawers would already be filled...with the clothes and memories of a little boy.

She'd been right about the desolate emptiness in Cole that had called to that same feeling inside her. Once, Cole had had a life, a family who loved him. Now he had an empty house and an empty soul, just like her.

The only difference was, she couldn't be sure she'd ever had a life with people who loved her. Cole at least had his memories...but perhaps, in a way, that made it even harder for him. She couldn't miss what she couldn't remember having.

If the dark, foreboding room that had flashed through her mind when Cole had first opened the door to his and Angela's bedroom was a part of her forgotten memories she wasn't sure she wanted to remember.

"HOW'S YOUR STEAK?" Cole asked. As they ate dinner at the small kitchen table, he was doing his best— which wasn't all that great—to find again the easy camaraderie they'd shared in the grocery store before he'd taken her upstairs and opened the doors to Angela's and Billy's rooms. It had been the first time he'd looked in either room since that awful night.

"Very good." She cut off a small piece of meat and chewed. That made a total of four bites, plus about the same number from her potato. For a short while, on the drive home and during their visit to the grocery store, she'd lost some of her tension. Her quiet voice and soft features had become animated as he'd teased her about her distinct preferences for foods she couldn't remember.

But then they'd arrived at his house and he'd frozen at the thought of her being inside the rooms that had belonged to Angela and Billy, as if simply by being there she would know about their lives and how he'd failed them. Of course, she'd sensed his mood...the change, the withdrawal, the fear...and her own mood had changed accordingly.

As he sat across the table from her, watching her nibble her food, he wondered if bringing her here had been a mistake, if he'd let his libido overrun his common sense. In the white cotton blouse and blue jeans, she somehow seemed even more fragile and more desirable than she had in the elegant wedding gown. And, just as he'd feared, he'd only made her feel worse.

She laid down her fork and looked at him squarely, her delicate features surprisingly resolute. "Perhaps it would be better if you took me back to the shelter. I feel like I'm intruding."

"No!" Maybe bringing her here had been a mistake, but he couldn't see taking her back to that shelter.

He didn't *want* to take her back to the shelter. He wanted her in his house, at his table, relaxed and smiling as she had been in the grocery store. He owed her that.

And more than responsibility, but he wasn't going to think about that now, about the tantalizing way she'd felt in his arms when he'd comforted her outside the morgue, the easy closeness they'd unexpectedly shared in the grocery store.

"You're not intruding," he assured her.

"Yes, I am. You kept those rooms closed until I came. I shouldn't be there."

He shook his head. "Of course you should be. They're rooms, unoccupied space. That's all. There just wasn't any reason to open them up until now." It should have been the truth, but it wasn't. He was lying, and he could tell she knew that.

"It bothered you to open the doors to those rooms."

"Yes," he agreed. He laid down his fork and gave up the pretense of eating. "It bothered me because I don't usually talk about Angela and Billy. I try to avoid even thinking about them."

She smiled weakly. "I suppose there are some advantages to having my memories taken away. I can't recall the painful things from my life."

"Yeah. That would be an advantage." But forgetting was something he'd never been able to do, something he wasn't entitled to do.

Silence dropped like a leaden weight between them. Mary picked up her fork and toyed with her potato.

"They were killed in an automobile accident." Cole forced himself to speak, to try to ease the tension and help her relax.

"That's terrible."

"Yeah, it was." She had no idea how terrible, and he wasn't about to tell her. Even if he'd wanted to…and he didn't…he wouldn't. She was already teetering on the edge. That could be just what it would take to push her over.

He was glad she'd elected to stay in Billy's room rather than the room he'd shared with Angela. He couldn't get over the feeling that that room might still hold some of Angela's essence and that essence would not only reveal to Mary his shortcomings, the truth about the accident, but would prey on her mind, blend with the dark fears that already filled the spaces where her memories had once lived and make everything worse.

"How old was Billy?"

"Eight." He picked up his empty beer can then set it down again. "I'm not doing too good at this conversation thing, am I? I guess it's just been too long."

She gave him a stronger smile then, albeit a sad one. "And I can't remember anything to make conversation about."

"Nothing at all? It's still a complete blank?"

She chewed her bottom lip as anxiety replaced the smile and creased her forehead. He resisted the urge to reach over and smooth away the creases. He might be able to make the physical gesture, but he couldn't smooth away whatever caused them.

"A couple of times I've had flashes, but I don't know if they're memories or just fears."

"What sort of flashes?"

"Upstairs when you first opened the door to yours and Angela's room, for an instant the room looked dim with dark, heavy furniture." She shrugged. "It was probably just my eyes adjusting to the brightness."

"Maybe not. Maybe that was a memory of your bedroom."

She shivered. "I hope not, because I was terrified to go into the room."

"What were you terrified of?"

"I don't know."

Had he been right? Had something of Angela remained behind to infect Mary, to make her paranoia worse?

Her chin lifted almost imperceptibly and her thin shoulders straightened though she clenched her hands on the table. "That's not the only time. When Officer

Townley called about the body, it brought up images of a knife and blood.'' She swallowed. ''What if I did kill someone? What if that's why I can't remember, because I can't face the fact that I'm a murderer?''

Cole studied her in silence for a long moment then shook his head. ''No way. You couldn't possibly have such a drastic personality change. I can't imagine you killing somebody, not even in self-defense.'' Actually, he couldn't imagine her defending herself. ''Pete told you about a guy who'd been stabbed, and you had a wedding dress with blood all over the front. Seems to me it would be pretty normal for that combination to bring up images of a knife and blood.''

''I hope that's all it was.''

''Maybe you ought to talk to a shrink, see if he can hypnotize you or do something to help bring back your memory.''

She looked down at her plate. ''Maybe. The doctor at the hospital said I should check back with him in a couple of days, but I'm not sure I need to. I feel okay physically.''

He wasn't surprised at her response. How could he expect her to have the courage to face her past when she didn't even have the courage to face the present?

Not that he had any right to be passing judgment. He couldn't face his own past.

He pushed back his chair and stood, gathering the dishes.

She rose also. ''Let me clean up. I can probably remember how to wash dishes.''

''I have a dishwasher, but I haven't used it since...since Angela died. It probably still works, though.''

They carried the dirty dishes over to the sink and

while Mary rinsed them, he went out the back door to check and be sure the charcoal he'd doused with water had stopped burning. Satisfied it had, he returned to the door, switched off the outside light, then stood for a moment before going in. The soft darkness with its chorus of tree frogs, crickets and other insects was soothing and suddenly he wanted to share that balm with Mary.

He stepped inside, closing only the screen door. "It's a beautiful night," he said. "Want to sit on the patio for a while?"

She looked up from adding detergent to the dishwasher and bit her lip.

Of course she wouldn't. That was dumb of him. Angela would never go outside after dark either. She said it made her feel too vulnerable, not being able to see what or who was around her. Naturally Mary would feel the same way.

But Mary's full lips firmed. "Yes," she said. "I'd like that." She closed the door to the dishwasher and adjusted the dials.

She started toward him, and the first cycle began with a click followed by a purring growl. She halted in midstep, her gaze becoming unfocused as a gentle dreaminess settled over her features.

Then she blinked away the fog, straightened and looked at him. "I think I almost had something then. I saw a big, sunny kitchen with yellow curtains at the windows. We were happy because the dishwasher worked."

"Who is *we?*" Her fiancé? Was she going to remember the man who'd given her the ring, the man she loved? An inexplicable tension gripped him at that thought.

"I'm not sure. I think it was my mother and father. I think my father had just installed the dishwasher." She laughed self-consciously. "I guess that's a pretty silly memory to retrieve."

"No. It sounds like a good memory to retrieve." Beat the hell out of blood and dark rooms. The wispy remnants of the pleasant memory clinging to her face beat the hell out of her usual pinched, fearful expression.

Even the harsh overhead light couldn't mar the soft blue of her eyes or the translucent blush that suffused her cheeks. The corners of her wide mouth tilted slightly upward and her white floral fragrance drifted to him. It must be a part of her since it was unlikely she'd remembered what kind of perfume she wore.

She'd always been beautiful, but now she was irresistible.

They stood scant inches apart, and all he would have to do to touch her was lean forward. He wasn't going to do that, of course. No matter how much he wanted her, he had no intention of doing that.

But he did.

Without quite knowing how it happened, he found himself reaching for her, pulling her slim body into his arms. She came to him without hesitation or surprise as if she, too, knew that this was the moment the whole day had been building toward. She fit perfectly against him, her breasts touching his chest, her heart beating against his. Her head tilted upward, lips slightly parted, eyes smoky and half-closed with desire. It was that last that stole any remaining fragment of common sense he might have had left.

His mouth moved slowly toward hers, savoring the

anticipation of the feel of those lips on his, of losing himself in the taste of her.

Suddenly she jerked backward, out of his arms, away from him. "What was that?"

He blinked and sucked in a quick breath, trying to orient himself, to fight his way up from the flood of desire that overwhelmed him. "What was what?" The fear was back in her eyes and her cheeks had lost their color.

She huddled against the counter. "I heard someone outside!"

He hadn't heard anything except the pounding of his own heart. "A 'possum or raccoon, maybe a deer. There are a lot of animals around here."

"No! It's—" Her wild gaze darted around the room and she lifted a shaky hand to her cheek.

"It's okay," he soothed, closing and locking the door behind him. "There's nobody out there."

Leaning against the counter, she tilted her head backward and closed her eyes as she drew in a deep breath. When she opened them again a moment later, her expression was calmer. "I did hear something," she said, and he could tell she was making a monumental effort to be calm.

"An animal."

She nodded. "Probably." She wrapped her arms around herself. "What if it was that man, that Sam Maynard?"

"It wasn't."

"You can't be positive of that."

"No," he admitted. "I can't be positive, but it's not likely. This place is hard to find even if you know it's here, and only a handful of people have my address. I went to a lot of trouble to make sure of that. Somebody like Sam Maynard who's not operating with a full deck anyway would never be able to find me. Besides, he wouldn't have any way of knowing that you're here with me. What you heard was only an animal.''

He watched her as he explained everything in a quiet, rational manner. She listened and nodded agreement, but the fear never left her eyes. He was no more able to reassure her than he'd been able to reassure Angela.

''I have an alarm system that I'll set before we go to bed. If anybody should try to come in a door or window, it will not only contact the security company, it will also make so much noise, the intruder will be deaf in five seconds.''

She smiled at his joke, but it wasn't a real smile.

''It's going to be okay,'' he said. ''I promise.'' Might as well promise to lasso the moon.

''I know.'' He could tell she didn't know any such thing.

He had to give her credit for guts, though he doubted if even that trait would be enough to conquer the demons that lived in her mind.

Chapter Five

Mary awoke early the next morning, surprised that she'd slept soundly and without dreams. Perhaps the nameless terror was finally vanquished, and without it filling the empty caverns of her mind, her memories might be able to return.

It was Sunday, the first day of the week, a day for beginnings. Maybe today she could begin to retrieve her past. Lying in the small bed with the sun filtering through the leaves of the big oak tree outside the window and touching her face, knowing that Cole was in a room down the hall, she felt ready. He made her feel safe and strong, as if she was able to absorb some of his courage.

She showered in the hall bath, using his soap, inhaling his scent, standing naked where he stood naked, and it was almost as if he were there, sharing his strength with her. But other, uninvited, less soothing, thoughts of him kept intruding…thoughts of him holding her and kissing her the way he would have last night if she hadn't panicked.

She set the soap aside and let the water skim over her body, rinsing away the lather. Maybe the panic had been a good thing after all. She'd wanted him to kiss her, wanted desperately to feel his lips on hers. Her wanting had driven out all common sense, such as the fact that she was engaged to another man, that she didn't know who she was, that Cole, who'd lived through his own personal hell and survived, could never be attracted to someone who was terrified of the world, even of the sounds of small animals in the night.

She toweled off and resolved not to think about that but to go downstairs, make breakfast and search for her memories, try to find the life she once had.

The kitchen was bright and open with a small window over the sink and a large bay window at the end where the table sat. Last night all that glass had been dark mirrors, reflecting back her own bleak spirit. This morning the windows revealed a forest of trees with sunlight dappling the leaves while birds and squirrels darted among them. A sassy cardinal perched on a limb and twisted his head as if peering in at her.

The woods were beautiful and dense, an effective screen from the outside world.

But they would also hide an intruder.

Stop it! She turned away from the window and ordered herself to ignore such thoughts, to hang on to her positive mood.

After she started the coffee, she found a skillet and put on some bacon then set the table. Delicious smells soon filled the kitchen, and she found herself humming as she searched for and found the ingredients to make biscuits. She couldn't remember her name but she could remember how to make biscuits, how to ensure they would be light and flaky, what temperature to set the oven, the way they'd taste with hot butter. None of this made any sense.

Unless you considered that biscuits were good memories.

No matter how much Cole tried to reassure her that her fears were of the unknown, that the images of blood had been called up by Officer Townley's description of the body, she couldn't shake the feeling that her mind was blocking something so awful she didn't want to remember it.

"GOOD MORNING."

The deep voice jerked Mary out of her pleasant fog, and she whirled around, temporarily sunblind, to see the silhouette of a man standing in the doorway. The egg she'd been about to crack fell from her nerveless fingers.

"Mary, it's me!" Cole moved toward her.

She drew a shaky hand across her forehead as her eyes adjusted. "I know," she lied. "You just startled me. That's all."

She grabbed a paper towel and stooped to clean up the egg that lay shattered on the floor. Cole squatted beside her, offering her another towel. His eyes were soft with sympathy and concern, and she hated that. Last night for a few moments he'd looked at her the way a man looks at a woman, and though she knew the futility of that avenue, she couldn't help but compare—and regret—the difference.

She stood, tossing the mess into the trash under the sink. "I really appreciate your letting me stay here," she said, making an effort to keep her voice strong and cheerful. "I slept soundly last night and didn't have nightmares. Probably because I feel safe here, I remember some more things." Surely the last part would please him.

"That's wonderful, Mary. Tell me what else you remember." Neither his voice nor his face revealed any expression.

"Last night the sound of the dishwasher triggered something. This morning it was the smells of coffee brewing and bacon frying." She turned her back to him and concentrated on beating the eggs with a wire whisk. "I recall waking up to those smells then lying in bed for a few minutes, listening to my mother and father talking in the kitchen. It gave me such a feeling of security." She poured the eggs into the skillet and stirred. "I lived on a farm in an old house. We didn't have a lot of money, and it was a big deal when we got that dishwasher. Dad gave it to mother for their fifteenth anniversary. He brought it home in the back of his pickup truck and it had a big red bow on top."

She lifted the skillet off the stove and turned around to spoon the eggs onto their plates.

Cole smiled at her, igniting an answering smile inside her breast. "That's great, Mary." He hesitated. "But that's probably not your name, is it?"

"I still don't know that." She set the skillet in the sink and took the biscuits out of the oven.

"Oh. How about your parents' names?"

She sighed. "Mom and Dad."

"I see."

She sank into a chair and added two spoons of sugar and a generous splash of cream to her coffee, stirred, then picked up her fork though she was no longer hungry. "That's right. No helpful details. I can see their faces, I can hear their laughter and feel their love for each other and for me. Dad's a tall man with dark hair and eyes. He works hard and sometimes he's too serious, but Mom can always make him smile. She's short and blond and totally dependent on him. We both are. He's very strong. He takes care of us. He likes to say that he'll do all the worrying while his two girls enjoy life.'' She shook her head in dismay. ''I know so much about them, but I don't know their names or my name or the name of the town where we lived. I guess I still don't know any more than I did yesterday.''

''Yes, you do. This is a breakthrough. And none of it's bad. You were so afraid it would be something terrible. Now you can stop worrying about that and maybe the rest will come faster.''

Mary nodded and nibbled on a piece of bacon. The memories of home and family had a nostalgic hue, like faded, treasured photographs. Anything could have happened between then and the present. But she wasn't going to admit that to Cole. She wasn't going to do anything to change the way he was looking at her with delight and approval.

''Don't worry,'' he assured her. ''You're getting a lot of details. Names should come soon.'' He drained the last of his coffee and set the cup on the table. ''I could try to trace your ring. With a stone that size, it shouldn't be too tough to find out where it came from.''

She shivered. The room seemed to darken as if a cloud had passed over the sun.

''I need to see if Pete will release your dress,'' Cole continued, oblivious to her distress. ''I'm sure he will since there's no evidence a crime has been committed. Then we can check with the local bridal shops and see if anybody has a record of selling it.''

Mary's mouth went suddenly dry. She lifted her coffee cup with fingers that trembled so badly she was barely able to drink from it. The brew was hot and bittersweet on her tongue, and she focused on that, avoiding the images of the ring and of the wedding dress stained with the blood of someone she couldn't remember. "Maybe he won't release the dress. Just in case something might come up."

"He'll have to. We can't hold personal items if there's no evidence of a crime."

"*We?*"

"What?"

"You said '*We* can't hold personal items.'"

Cole grimaced. "Habit. I used to be a cop for a lot of years. Pete was my partner." He rose from the table and walked over to pour another cup of coffee.

"You used to be a policeman?" A shiver darted down her spine.

His reply seemed ordinary enough. She supposed a lot of private investigators were former police officers. Yet she could tell from his tone that it wasn't ordinary to him, nor was it ordinary to her. She wanted nothing to do with policemen.

From the beginning, no matter how kind Officer Townley had been to her, she'd never felt she could trust him. The feeling was completely illogical and had to come from something in her past, some reason that compelled her to distrust and avoid policemen. Was this further evidence that she had committed a crime, perhaps murder?

"Yeah," Cole said. "I was with the Dallas Police Department for twelve years. You want some more coffee?"

"Yes, please." Apparently he didn't want to talk about his years in uniform, and she didn't want him to. What secrets lurked in both their pasts to cause such inexplicable reactions?

He refilled her cup then sat down across from her again. "Since it's Sunday, there's not a lot we can do as far as the dress and the ring. Do you feel up to driving around the area where I ran into you? See if it jogs your memory?"

She didn't ever want to go back there, but she wasn't going to admit it. "I stayed in that hotel near there for two days and that didn't help." She'd never ventured outside the hotel, had only left her room to go down to the coffee shop for meals, but she couldn't admit that to Cole.

"That was before your memory started returning. Could be that a familiar sight now would be the key to everything, like the familiar sounds last night and the smells this morning."

She stirred more sugar into her coffee, the spoon moving faster and faster, creating a dark whirlpool that invited her to plunge into its bottomless depths and escape.

The liquid sloshed over the side of the cup, onto the table.

"Oh!" She shot to her feet, grabbed her napkin and tried to blot up the mess. "I'm so clumsy this morning!"

"It's okay," Cole soothed. "Don't worry about it. Sit down and relax."

She fell into her chair in dismay. That sympathetic tone was back in his voice and on his face.

"We don't have to go anywhere," he assured her in that same voice.

"Yes, we do. I need to. I want to." She tilted her chin upward and concentrated on making her gaze steady as she met his head-on. The effort took all the strength she had and some she hadn't known she possessed, but it was worth it. The look in Cole's eyes changed to one of admiration.

"I've got an idea," he said. "Why don't we take a picture of you, scan it into my computer and print out some posters to put up in the buildings in the area? I know your picture was in every area newspaper and on every news broadcast, but there are people who don't read papers or watch the news."

She swallowed hard, forcing down the *No!* that wanted to come out of her mouth, ignoring the strangling fingers of fear that wrapped around her throat. "Good idea," she said.

COLE DROVE his beloved T-bird along the winding streets of the Oak Lawn and Turtle Creek areas. The day was beautiful and he had the top down since it was still early enough that the sun didn't feel like a blast furnace.

Mary sat beside him with the wind tossing her moonlight hair in the bright sunlight. She seemed to be a part of the wind and sunlight, so fragile she could float away at any minute. He had to resist the urge to take her arm and hold her down, keep her with him. That would be as futile as trying to grasp a sunbeam. Mary wasn't really *with him* anyway, and the small part that was could leave at any minute.

Even so, he had to applaud her effort to be brave. He knew this project terrified her, though she smiled and talked while one hand clutched the door and the other was knotted in a fist in her lap, the bruises on her wrist a dark, ominous stain. He had some misgivings about this trip, but now that she'd started remembering, he wanted to be with her when the rest came back.

And he'd wanted to get her out of the house.

If he were completely honest with himself, he'd have to admit that the thought of spending the entire day alone in the house with her tantalized him to the point that he knew one or both of them needed to get out. Last night he'd come far too close to kissing her. He could tell she felt the same desire for him as he did for her, and that made the situation doubly appealing and doubly dangerous.

She was too delicate. He had to be careful with her. He knew from experience that what she wanted from him was more than passion, more than holding each other through the night. She wanted safety, the one thing he couldn't give.

Getting out today, looking around and putting up posters was the best idea he'd been able to come up with.

He pulled into the empty parking lot of an office building, one of the two she'd appeared between. "Here we are."

"Yes," she agreed. "Here we are." She flung open her door and slid out as if afraid she'd change her mind if she waited.

Today she wore a pair of khaki shorts that revealed long, slim legs. Like her face and arms, her legs were translucent porcelain, untouched by the sun's rays. He couldn't help but wonder if that meant she'd always been fearful of the world, if she'd spent her time behind locked doors and drawn curtains.

As they went around to the front of the building, he had to clench his fists to keep from taking her hand. She seemed to float rather than walk, the quality emphasizing the ethereal air that both attracted and frightened him, and, as in the car, he felt the need to hold on to her, to keep her from drifting away.

He couldn't. He knew that. He could only frustrate himself and then feel guilty because he'd been unable to help.

"That's where you first appeared," he said, pointing to the grassy area between the two buildings.

She looked up, her gaze scanning the structures as if she expected one of the store gargoyles to fly down and attack her. Finally she licked her lips, straightened her spine and walked determinedly between them.

They checked every building on that block as well as every block that bordered it, went inside whenever possible, taped or nailed posters to any available surface, and always Mary shook her head.

"I can't," she finally said, crossing her arms under her breasts and squinting into the sun as she turned to face him. "I don't recognize anything. I know I should, but maybe I can't because I don't want to."

"It's okay," he said, and was surprised to find that he wasn't as disappointed as he should have been. Perhaps he, too, didn't want to know about her past, a past that could include a crime and certainly included a fiancé. "Let's go get some lunch and drive around the city, stop at a couple of the big malls. Maybe you'll recognize a favorite restaurant or a store where you've shopped."

She nodded, her expression bleak and without hope.

He chose a small Mexican restaurant in the area. It was after two o'clock, and only a few tables were occupied. Mary hesitated briefly at the door, her head moving slightly from one side to the other as if she was scanning the faces. The action was so short and her steps so sure as she entered the place that he'd have missed it if he hadn't known what to watch for.

"How about a table up front so you can look through the window and see if anyone goes by that you recognize?"

She wavered for a moment but then shook her head. "They could see me, too. I can't. I'm sorry."

"No problem. We'll ask for a table in the back."

He wasn't surprised that her willpower was used up. A little disappointed, maybe, but not surprised.

The hostess seated them at a booth in the rear where the lighting was dim, as far as possible from the plate-glass window.

"I'm sorry," Mary said again. "The thought of being so exposed was scary."

"No problem," he said again. "You've had a stressful morning." And if he pushed her any harder, she would surely shatter just as that egg had shattered on the floor when he'd startled her earlier.

Cole ordered a beer and Mary asked for a glass of iced tea.

The waitress returned shortly with their drinks along with a basket of tortilla chips and a bowl of salsa, then took their orders.

Mary asked for extra jalapeños with her enchiladas, then proceeded to stir two packets of sugar into her tea. Cole leaned back against the padded plastic and chuckled. "A country music fan, a woman who bakes biscuits from scratch, drinks sweetened iced tea and eats jalapeños. At least we know for sure you're a Texan."

Mary's tense features relaxed one muscle at a time, the result a soft smile. "It's a big state. I'm not sure that narrows down the search very much."

"But it does bring up a possibility. You said you

grew up on a farm. Maybe you don't live in Dallas but in one of the surrounding areas. That could be why nobody's come forward to identify you. They may not have had access to the story on television or in the newspaper."

"I've been gone four days and nobody's missed me, nobody's checked with the authorities? That doesn't seem very likely."

"Maybe not, but it could happen. You might have planned to take a few days to come into Dallas and shop for your wedding dress."

Mary twirled her straw in the pale amber tea and smiled wryly. "When the alteration lady stuck me with a pin, I killed her?"

"You keep saying you killed somebody. There's absolutely no evidence to support that theory. You could have been present at the scene of some sort of accident."

"A really bad accident, judging from the blood."

"Not necessarily. Someone could have fallen and hit his head. Head wounds bleed a lot."

She considered that for a moment. "If I'd tried to help, that would explain the blood on my dress."

"Right."

She wrapped both hands around her cool glass of tea and looked at him with pleading in her eyes, begging him to convince her of that scenario. "But why would that be so horrible I wouldn't want to remember it?"

For someone as fragile as Mary, he could well imagine that seeing such an accident would send her into a total state of shock and amnesia. But he wouldn't tell her that. "Maybe the person died." Maybe it was her fiancé.

"Then why wasn't it reported?"

"Okay, he didn't die."

"He didn't show up in a hospital, either. Officer Townley said they checked and found no accident victims with AB-positive blood who knew anything about me."

"There are hundreds of neighborhood clinics around town, some more reputable than others, where he could have gone to be patched up." If she wanted him to convince her, she needed to stop coming up with such valid arguments. He selected a chip and drew it through the salsa then ate it and took a big drink of his beer.

She followed his lead, and they munched on chips and salsa for a couple of minutes.

"What if it wasn't an accident?" she asked. "What if I witnessed a murder? That would explain why the body hasn't shown up. The murderer hid it."

She spoke almost dispassionately, as if discussing a movie she'd seen or something that had happened to an acquaintance. The terror that usually permeated every word and every glance was still there but to a much lesser degree. Perhaps the known, no matter how awful, was less terrifying than the unknown, or perhaps she'd simply reached her mind's limits of coping with fear.

"The murderer could be looking for me," she continued in that same disconnected tone. "I could be the next victim."

She was right. That was a possible scenario and would explain a lot. So maybe she had reason to be paranoid. Maybe he'd misjudged her.

"If that's what happened, I promise you won't be the next victim," he assured her. If the threat was real, if it came in the form of a flesh-and-blood person, he could protect her. "I did learn a few things in my years on the police force."

"Why did you leave the force?"

Her innocent question stole the brief surge of confidence.

Fortunately the waitress arrived at that moment with their food, and he had a chance to think about his answer, to hope she'd forget the question.

They ate in silence for a few moments, and he was pleased to notice that she was eating more. He'd begun to fear for her physical well-being as much as her mental.

She finished one enchilada and most of her beans, then pushed her plate away. "I didn't mean to pry," she said. "When I asked why you left the force, I mean. You don't have to tell me. It's none of my business."

"Burnout," he said curtly.

"I see."

He didn't know if the amnesia had robbed her of her defenses or if her thoughts and feelings had always shown so clearly on her face and in her eyes. Whichever it was, he could tell now that she did, indeed, understand his answer all too well; that she knew he didn't want to talk about it and that she would honor that need.

He felt ashamed, almost as if he had lied to her, certainly as if he owed her something more. Not the whole truth, but at least a part of it. She trusted him enough to stay in his house, to put her safety in his hands, and yet she knew absolutely nothing about him because he didn't trust her with himself.

He shoved his half-eaten plate aside. Suddenly he no longer had an appetite.

"After Angela and Billy were killed, I couldn't do it anymore," he said. "If I wasn't able to keep my own family safe, what the hell was I doing on the streets trying to keep other people safe?"

"Were you with your family when they...when the accident happened?"

He sighed and leaned back, draping his arm along the back of the seat and looking across the room. Through the plate-glass window he could see the world outside where people passed, normal people who still had their souls intact, unlike Mary and him. She'd lost hers somewhere in the dark recesses of her mind, and his had shriveled and died three years ago.

"I wasn't with them," he replied, still not looking at her, not meeting her gaze. "I was at work, on a stakeout. Angela was...upset that night. She called me several times, but I couldn't leave to go home. So she and Billy got in the car and left the house. She ran a red light and plowed into a semi truck. They were both killed instantly. Fortunately, nobody else was hurt."

He dared to look at her then, into those trusting, guileless eyes, to see if she noticed the gaps in that story, gaps huge enough to drive that semi through. What he saw was sympathy, an echo of his pain, and for a moment a current flowed between the two of them.

He blinked and looked away. He didn't want or deserve her sympathy, and he could do nothing to assuage her pain. Or his.

"That must have been awful," she said softly.

"Yeah, it was." He picked up the ticket and rose. "Ready to go check out the rest of the city?"

"All right."

Before they'd entered the restaurant, the temperatures had risen to a point where riding in the convertible was no longer comfortable. Now the sun beat down mercilessly, and Cole raised the top on his car.

As they drove around Dallas, Mary, while still clenching her hands in her lap, nevertheless seemed to sit straighter, to hold her head higher. He wouldn't call her relaxed, but she was less tense. Part of it could stem from her fears of being seen. Now that he'd put up the top, she was somewhat hidden from the world.

But he sensed it was more than that. With his partial admission of the torment in his own soul, they'd turned a corner of some sort. It was almost as if she now knew that she couldn't depend on him and would have to rely on her own strength and, consequently, was finding more of that strength.

"The Galleria!" she exclaimed as they drove along LBJ Freeway past the large shopping mall. "I remember the Galleria!" She turned to him with a wide, expectant smile.

"Galleria, here we come!" He steered for the nearest exit, circled around and pulled into the parking lot of the shopping center. When they parked, she merely continued to stare and made no move to get out of the car.

"Do you want to go in?" he asked.

She nodded. "Of course. It's just that—"

"You're scared."

"Yes, but that's not it. There's something about the mall that's not quite right."

"Maybe you're not used to parking on this side. Let's go in. You'll probably recognize some of the shops. This could be where your ring and gown came from."

The mention of those two items caused the usual

return of tension, but she opened her door and got out wordlessly anyway.

The parking lot was crowded with people hurrying in every direction, pushing past, rushing to get home or just out of the heat. For the most part, their gazes were turned inward, focused on their own lives, though some stared openly at Mary. She was, after all, a beautiful woman. Her eyes darted back and forth as if she was searching every face that came into range.

He took her arm to guide her, to make her feel safe and because he wanted to touch her. He could feel her flinch every time someone brushed past or looked directly at her. He could also feel the stilted movement of her stride, as if she had weights attached to her feet. But she never once hesitated, pushing on past her fears until they reached the entrance.

The mall was more crowded than the parking lot, and they made slow progress as Mary scanned each face and each storefront. She hesitated in front of Saks Fifth Avenue but then moved on. Cole spotted a bridal boutique and, with one hand at her waist to support her just in case, urged her toward it. "Think you might have bought your dress there?"

To his surprise, she didn't freak, but merely stood there shaking her head. "I don't know. We can go in and check."

The clerk at the shop showed them pictures of recently sold gowns, but none was similar to Mary's. Cole wasn't surprised. He suspected she would have reacted in some way if it had been the right shop.

Finally as they paused to watch ice skaters whirling on the indoor rink, she turned to him and shook her head. "We might as well leave. This isn't accomplishing anything."

She was silent on the way home, and he didn't intrude on her thoughts. Her gaze stayed focused out the window as if she was searching for something. Her past, he supposed.

When they reached his front door, he unlocked the dead bolt and disabled the burglar alarm.

"I'm sorry," she said.

He paused with his hand on the doorknob and reflected that she used that expression frequently. "What are you sorry for?"

She shrugged. "Everything. Not being able to recognize the buildings, being afraid to sit up front in the restaurant, not recognizing the mall." She frowned and bit her lip. "The Galleria was so familiar and yet not familiar at the same time. The place nags at the edges of my memory, like when you hear a few words from a song, and you know the song, but you can't quite catch the melody or remember any more of the lyrics."

"You may think you haven't accomplished anything today, but you have. Think about it. Over the course of twelve hours, you've recovered memories of your parents and you got up the courage to go out in public, to start searching for your past. You've come a long way since you dropped that egg when I walked in this morning."

"And spilled my coffee." She smiled up at him, standing so close to him on the porch that her elusive scent of white flowers mingled with the fresh green fragrance of the surrounding canopy of trees. A robin trilled overhead and from somewhere in the depths of the woods, a blue jay squawked.

The waning afternoon sunlight dappled her quicksilver hair as it hung softly about her shoulders and draped her face. Despite her smile, in her eyes he could see the sadness and regret of what she seemed to consider her failure, and more than anything, he wanted to make that sadness and regret disappear.

He lifted a hand to cup her cheek. ''Ease up on yourself. You've come a long way in the last three days. Just take it one step at a time.''

Her unguarded eyes, the clear color of the sky overhead, filled with gratitude, and he realized that he'd just lied to himself. What he really wanted to do more than anything was to kiss her. Twice before he'd been this close and pulled away, but he couldn't do it a third time. No matter how much he knew he should, no matter how concerned he was about her vulnerability or the unknown fiancé that waited for her. All those concerns were shoved to the back of his mind by his need for her.

He wasn't sure if he pulled her into his arms or if she flowed there, but suddenly her body was clinging to his, her head lifted to offer him her mouth, the blue of her half-closed eyes smoky and inviting. Her lips on his were soft and firm and warm and moist, and though her body felt fragile in his arms, she pressed against him and returned his kiss with an intensity of passion that surprised and aroused him and made him hungry for more, so much more.

The world around them vanished, leaving nothing but the two of them, her lips on his, her body slim and supple in his arms, her breasts against his chest, her heart beating wildly in time with his, the rhythm strong and steady. He wanted her, all of her, wanted to carry her inside the house, up to his room, lay her across his bed and make love to her all night, become a part of her, the only reality she knew and the only reality that mattered right now.

And then it was over.

Gently she eased away from him, her hands on his shoulders, her lips red and swollen from their kiss, her breath coming in ragged pants. "We probably ought to go inside," she said, her voice husky.

If she hadn't been strong enough to pull away, they'd be going inside, all right. Straight to his bedroom. In this instance at least, she was stronger than he.

He opened the door and she preceded him inside.

She had come a long way in one day. He'd given in completely to his hormones, his need for her overriding his concern for her needs. He'd almost taken advantage of her vulnerability. If this was his idea of caring for her, being responsible, he needed to rearrange his thinking.

Now all he had to do was get through the rest of the evening with her and all the night, knowing she was sleeping only a few feet away.

Oh, yeah! He was doing really great on the responsibility issue. Not one damn bit better than last time.

Worse, in fact. He'd never been so out of control with Angela. She'd had nothing to fear from him, only from what he couldn't do.

But Mary was another matter entirely. He'd caused or at least contributed to her problem, and he'd do the best he could for her...reassure her, keep the house locked and hope her fiancé rescued her soon. That was all he could do. He could lock the monsters outside, but at the same time, he'd be locking in the ones that lived in her mind...and he'd be locking her in with his desire for her.

The best he could hope for was that she would wake in the morning with perfect recall. Then she could return to her home and her fiancé, someone who could care for her and keep her safe.

Except her mysterious fiancé hadn't done a very good job of it so far.

The alternative was that she could wake in the morning and remember witnessing a murder. Then she'd become the responsibility of the police department. All she'd need to do would be to tell the police, and when they caught the murderer, she could return to her normal, safe life. If it was possible for someone with her soul-deep terrors to return to a normal, safe life after witnessing something as horrible as a murder.

For a moment he couldn't decide if he wanted her to remember or not, if he wished her back in the life that had produced such fear.

But that brought him full circle to the final alternative…that she never regained her memory, that she was dependent on him to keep her from harm, to pull her back from the abyss. He'd known he wasn't capable of that job before he'd kissed her. Now he wasn't even sure he could save himself.

She had to regain her memory.

He awakened the next morning to the sound of a woman screaming.

Chapter Six

Mary slammed the front door closed and leaned on the solid wood, her heart pounding erratically, the darkness beating against the windows of her mind in its effort to get in, to suck her down into the bottomless, painless, safe void.

"Mary!" He grabbed her, and she screamed again, trying to push him away, but his grip on her wrists was like a steel band.

"What's the matter? What happened?"

She shook her head, not wanting to think about any of it, only wanting to get away from him, seek the solace of the beckoning blackness. But he held her close against his chest, and the clean scent of soap mingled with a familiar masculine essence that suffused her nostrils and pulled her back.

Cole.

It was Cole who held her.

She'd done it again, completely lost control, gone off into her nightmare realm. She couldn't lift her head, couldn't look into his face and see again the pity. He stroked her back soothingly, the way a father would do for a frightened child, not the way a man did for a desirable woman...not the way he'd touched her last night when he'd held her and kissed her and she'd felt like a real person.

"What's the matter, Mary? What happened?"

She forced herself to look up, to meet his gaze as if she hadn't just made a total fool of herself. "I thought I heard something outside, so I opened the door." She swallowed the bile that rose in her throat. "There's blood on the porch. An animal. It's…dead."

He moved her gently aside and opened the door. "It's a rabbit," he said. "I'll take care of it."

She wanted to call him back, to beg him not to leave her alone, but that was foolish and weak and she was tired of being foolish and weak, of having Cole see her that way, of seeing herself that way.

Her brief glimpses into her past told her that she had not lived her entire life as a timid, fearful person. At one time she had been normal. Something must have happened to cause this change.

When she'd first awakened with no memories, she'd thought her terror came from the emptiness, from the sensation of being alone in a strange world without even her past as a companion. But now she had a few of those memories back, happy memories, and still the terror ruled her life.

What had happened to create so much fear, to make her want to escape from her past into nothingness?

She knew with a dreadful certainty that it had something to do with her wedding, with the gown and the ring.

And, of course there was the blood.

Again the unwelcome thought returned…had she harmed her fiancé in some way, maybe even killed him? Had she witnessed her fiancé's murder? Was her life in danger from his killer?

Somehow she had to find the courage to face her past, to confront whatever it was that had happened, no matter how awful it was.

When they'd shared that mind-shattering kiss last night, Cole had seemed to imbue her not only with his passion but also with his strength. For that one moment, he'd made her feel alive and given her an identity. But it couldn't have meant the same for him. He felt a responsibility for her. She couldn't imagine that someone as weak and needy as she could arouse passion in a man as strong as Cole. The kiss had probably been incidental to him.

But it had not been incidental to her. The memory of the exhilaration when his lips touched hers, of the sense of completeness that had wrapped around her, gave her something to hold on to.

She knew it shouldn't be that way. Somewhere in her life she had made a promise to another man, a promise she should keep even if she couldn't remember making it. And even if that were not true, she knew she was not the kind of woman Cole needed.

Nevertheless, she found herself searching every inch of her being, trying to find the courage to face her life, present and past, to beat back the darkness and become someone Cole would look at with respect and desire, someone he'd want to kiss again, even if it never happened.

When he returned a few minutes later, she was in the kitchen, making breakfast.

"There are a lot of predators in the woods...coyotes, owls, even some feral cats," he said, watching her carefully as if he expected her to collapse. "I'm sorry you had to see that."

"It's okay. I overreacted. It was the blood." Far too

much blood for a rabbit, but she didn't say that. "I may have to become a vegetarian." She put all her efforts into giving him a smile.

"It was pretty gruesome," Cole admitted. "Nature can be cruel. Anybody would have been shocked to open the door to a sight like that."

He was giving her an excuse, but she refused to take it. Maybe she'd never regain her memory, never know who she'd been and never know what horrible event or even what minor event had caused her to discard her life. But one thing she did know, she didn't like being the terrified, lost creature who'd awakened on the pavement four days ago, the person who jumped at every noise and wanted only to retreat again into the black void of forgetfulness.

When Cole suggested after breakfast that she go with him to reclaim the bridal gown from the police department, she clenched her teeth against the swirling terror before it could secure its grip on her.

"I can't ask you to do that," she protested. "I'm sure you have work that needs to be done." What she said was true, even though her real reluctance came from the fear generated by even a mention of that dress.

"I've checked my workload. I don't have anything that has to be done for a few days. That's one of the few perks of this business…keeping my own hours." He slid his chair back from the table. "Let me call Pete and be sure he can meet us."

She nodded then set about loading the dishwasher, concentrating fiercely on the simple task in order to avoid concentrating on that dress she would soon have to confront. She couldn't recall anything about it—not the style, the fabric, the fit—nothing except the way the blood had soaked through and clung to her skin, the coppery smell, the dark color.

"He's not in the office yet," Cole said. "I left a message. I'm going upstairs to shower. Would you grab the phone if it rings?"

"All right."

She had just finished wiping off the table, when a shrill ring stabbed the quiet house. Predictably, her heart began to race.

Stupid! she berated herself, tossing the sponge into the sink. *It's only the telephone!*

Even so, her stiff legs dragged feet of concrete as she entered the living room and crossed to the lamp table where the phone sat. Before lifting the receiver, she glanced at the readout on the caller ID box.

Anonymous. Her breath came in ragged gulps and she had to fight for control.

It's only Pete. Police officers frequently used that device. Another bit of trivia she wasn't sure how she knew but was nevertheless certain of.

"Hello?"

"Mary? This is Pete. Cole around?"

One point for her. She'd faced a fear and found it to be a fraud. "He's taking a shower."

"I'm just getting ready to leave the house. Would you tell him I'll get your dress and meet you all at the station in an hour?"

"I will. Thanks, Pete."

She smiled as she replaced the receiver. She'd thanked him not for the promise to return a dress she never wanted to see again but for proving to her that her fears could be groundless, products of a mind in limbo with no reality to hang on to.

The phone rang a second time and she unhesitantly

reached for the receiver. The caller ID again said *anon-ymous*. Perhaps Pete had forgotten something.

"Hi, Pete," she said, heady with her newfound courage.

A long silence greeted her.

"Hello?" she said tentatively.

"Those who truly love will always forgive no matter how grave the sin."

Mary slammed the phone down, her temporary courage sucked away into the depths of that hoarse whisper.

"Was that Pete?"

She whirled around to see Cole walking down the stairs, buttoning his denim shirt over his broad chest. She opened her mouth to speak but no sound came out. In spite of her resolutions, the fear had once again stolen her soul.

With a monumental effort, she cleared her throat and forced herself to rise through it. "Pete called," she managed to say. "He'll meet us in an hour."

Cole reached the bottom of the stairs and looked at her curiously. He must have heard the phone ring a second time, heard her answer then saw her hang up without saying goodbye.

"Someone else called," she explained.

"Who?"

"I don't know."

"Hang-up call?"

"No. It was…a man, I think. He said—" She drew in a deep breath and made herself repeat the innocent words that somehow seemed menacing. "'Those who truly love will always forgive no matter how grave the sin.'"

Cole's eyes narrowed and his lips tightened as he checked the caller ID. But then he shrugged. "Probably some religious nut calling at random. My number's un-listed.''

His voice was as casual as the shrug, but he didn't meet her gaze as he spoke, and his shoulders seemed tense.

Or was her imagination working overtime? The dead rabbit had frightened her, set her up to see innocent events in a threatening light.

Cole was probably right in his assessment of the call. In fact, maybe she hadn't really heard the words at all. Maybe her confused brain had conjured them up from the dark silence on the other end of the phone, some memory from out of the black hole that was her life.

Neither possibility could harm her. She had to stop being afraid of shadows. Cole had done it. He might be tormented by the memory of his wife and son, but he feared nothing.

She could never imagine Cole being afraid, but something had happened, something more than the horrible automobile accident that had taken the lives of his wife and son, something that had turned any remaining softness in him to tempered steel. She needed to learn how to do that herself.

As THEY WALKED into the police station to meet Pete, past the receptionist and back to the area where the officers had their desks, Mary cringed. Heads lifted and eyes turned toward them, and she had to fight the sensation that everyone had been talking about her in a derogatory manner, censuring her. Even though she could label the feeling as paranoia, she couldn't make it go away.

The building was old and she could detect faint smells of cigarette smoke, strong coffee and the starch of police uniforms. She fancied she could smell…or maybe it was only sense…the sweaty fear of murderers. It was all vaguely familiar and disquieting.

"Grayson, you old dog!" Several of the officers came over to clap Cole on the back and shake his hand.

"Where you been hiding?"

"Change your mind about coming to work again?"

Of course they'd all been looking. They remembered Cole from his time on the force. At least she hadn't imagined that part…just the reason for their interest. Once more, for no discernible reason, she'd given in to her fears.

"I'm Joe Franklin," one officer said, smiling broadly as he extended a hand to Mary. "What's a beautiful woman like you doing hanging out with an ugly creep like this guy?"

Mary tensed at the man's teasing. These people assumed she was a friend of Cole's, not just a woman with no memory on whom he'd taken pity.

"Hey, watch it or I'll have to reshape your face so even your dog won't have anything to do with you!" Cole retorted, smiling as he wrapped a protective arm around her waist, and for a single instant she felt as if she belonged, as if she had an identity.

"Hey, Grayson!" Pete strode up, carrying a large plastic bag with the folded bridal gown inside. "How's it going, Mary? Hope this helps you figure things out."

She accepted the bag from him, clutching it by two corners, holding it away from her, avoiding as much contact as possible.

She fancied she could feel the atmosphere thicken and congeal as everyone realized who she was, that she wasn't a real person after all.

"You're the bride!" Joe exclaimed, then looked a

little embarrassed. "So, is, uh, everything okay now? That weirdo's been in here looking for you again. He's not bothering you, is he?"

The walls seemed to shrink, to close in around her as the air was sucked from the room, making it hard to get her breath.

Cole took the bag from her as his other arm tightened reassuringly around her waist. "What weirdo? Sam the Sleaze?"

"Yeah, him. Well, Pete can tell you all about it."

Pete scowled at Joe, who retreated to his desk. "There's not a lot to tell. You know Sam. When he starts obsessing about a woman, he obsesses until he meets the next one."

"Let's go to your office and talk about it," Cole suggested.

He propelled her along as they followed Pete to a small room containing three chairs as well as a desk almost covered by a computer and several mounds of papers. Pete took the chair behind the desk and motioned them to the others. Mary sank onto the cold plastic surface with relief. She hadn't lost control, but she was hanging on to it by tattered fingernails.

Cole tossed the dress onto Pete's desk and remained standing. "You guys have hauled that creep in here so many times, he's as familiar with the place as any of us," he said. "You think there's any chance he could have found my address?"

"Of course not! The only place your address would be is in your personnel file."

Cole flopped into the other chair and cocked one foot onto the edge of Pete's desk, then looked at Mary as if unsure how much he should say.

She licked her dry lips. "The rabbit," she said.

"You think maybe he brought the rabbit, don't you? There was far too much blood to have come from that small animal."

Cole listened to Mary's description with surprise. He hadn't realized she'd noticed the excess blood, and he certainly hadn't wanted to mention it to her. That went a long way toward explaining her hysteria that morning.

"What rabbit?" Pete asked.

"It was on the front porch this morning," Cole explained. "Could have been meant to scare Mary, an effort to keep her from regaining her memory. Or it could have been just one of those freaky things that happens when you have lots of animals around." He made every effort to sound casual, to downplay the incident as much as possible in order to allay Mary's fears.

Pete shook his head. "That doesn't sound like Sam. Too much work for him. Too much logic." He, too, cast Mary a tentative look, but then continued. "All right, here's the latest poop. He came in early this morning wearing a black suit he must have found in a Dumpster somewhere. Sure smelled like it. Said he wanted to invite all of us to his wedding, that his bride was waiting at the church. Showed us a picture of you that he'd cut from the newspaper."

Mary clenched her hands in her lap. "This morning someone called right after your call. He said something strange about loving and forgiving." Cole could hear the tension in her voice, but she was making a laudable effort to sound normal. "And don't forget the hang-up call at the hotel. Maybe that man does know how to access your information. Maybe he knows where Cole lives and what his phone number is. Maybe he knows every move I make.'' Her voice rose slightly on the last sentence.

Pete shook his head. ''Not likely. He's got way too many screws loose.''

''Stranger things have happened,'' Cole said.

''Yeah, I guess they have.''

''Anything else happening on Mary's case?''

Pete's gaze flickered over Mary then quickly darted away, and he shook his head, his expression slightly guilty.

''Where are you at in this investigation?'' Cole demanded.

Pete spread his hands in a helpless gesture. ''Come on, man. You were on the force. You know how it works. There's no evidence that a crime's been committed. What are we going to investigate? Uncovering Mary's identity is a civil matter. We don't have enough manpower to cover all the murders, robberies and drug deals as it is.''

Cole nodded. ''Yeah, I know.'' But the rules shouldn't apply to Mary, not when she needed help so desperately. ''I think I'll pay Sam a visit.''

Pete's eyes narrowed, and Cole knew exactly what his former partner was thinking. What's more, he knew Pete could be right, probably was right. The odds were minimal that Sam Maynard had been able to find Cole's home and unlisted phone number and had then gone to the trouble to make a strange phone call and leave a dead rabbit.

But he was no longer so certain that all of Mary's fears came from inside her own mind or that he wouldn't be able to help her. Something had happened that involved human blood, the blood on her wedding gown. However, the bloody rabbit on his doorstep could have been a freak accident. The strange phone call could have been the work of a religious nut. Both incidents could be unrelated to the blood on her wedding gown.

Or they could be related. If she had witnessed a murder, the murderer could be stalking her.

Though finding Cole's house and unlisted phone number would not have been easy.

At this point, he didn't have sufficient evidence even to venture a guess concerning the situation.

The only thing he knew for certain was that Mary was making a major effort on her own. He was aware that she hadn't wanted to come to the station, hadn't wanted to see that dress again and certainly didn't want to talk about that rabbit. But she'd forced herself to do all those things.

In the face of her courage, he had no choice. He would do whatever he could to help, and the first thing was to eliminate Sam's perversions as a possibility.

After that, he'd use all his detective skills to help her recover her memories. He had to know what enemy threatened her and whether there was any hope that he could help her defeat that enemy. In the face of her courage and, more importantly, after that kiss they'd shared last night, he had to know. If the enemy came from inside, he couldn't kiss her or hold her or become any more involved with her than he already was. In that event, he'd have to admit that he couldn't help her.

But if the enemy was real and tangible and if he could help her defeat that enemy, maybe he'd be able to recapture part of his own soul.

Of course, helping her recover her memories would also mean finding the man who'd given her the ring she hated. And that was something else he needed to do…especially after that kiss.

THAT AFTERNOON Cole pulled up in front of the run-down house where Sam Maynard lived, behind the big old gray car registered in his name. The man was intermittently employed as a day laborer, but the car indicated he was home. Lucky, because Cole didn't want to have to come back.

He'd had a tough time convincing Mary that she should stay at his place while he came here alone. He could tell she really didn't want to come, didn't want to face the man who might be stalking her, but she had been grimly determined to do it. Once again he had to admire her courage. She was a fighter.

The first time he had had occasion to come here several years ago, he'd been surprised to find the small house tidy and well kept. But Sam's mother, Grace Maynard, had still been alive then. She'd died and left the place to Sam five years ago, and weeds now vied for space with the remnants of a flower garden. The screen door hung askew on its hinges, and cardboard had been nailed inside a broken windowpane.

Cole strode up the cracked walk and across the rickety porch. From inside the house he could hear a radio tuned to a hard-rock station. He knocked on the door and waited, not surprised when no one answered. He lifted a fist and banged loudly on the door. It swung slowly open.

He was no longer a cop, no longer constrained by rules and regulations, just an ordinary citizen who could consider himself invited in when a door opened. He walked inside.

The small living room was musty and dim, the furniture old and dark. A framed portrait in the middle of the coffee table, surrounded by beer cans and fast-food wrappers, caught his eye and he did a double take. For just a moment, in the dim light, he'd thought it was a picture of Mary holding a baby.

He snatched it up and looked closer. The picture was old and the woman bore only a superficial resemblance to Mary.

He set it down and looked around, noting that other photographs were scattered around the room, some framed, others leaning against lamps, ashtrays or even beer cans. The progression of years captured in the images revealed the woman to be Sam's mother, Grace. Well, at least the man had loved his mother.

"Maynard!" he called, following the sound of the music down a short hallway.

The music stopped.

Still wearing the black suit Pete had described, Maynard burst out of one of the bedrooms. "What are you doing here? Get out! Get out! You can't come in here!" Strands of thin, greasy hair bounced about his large head.

Cole raised his hands in a conciliatory gesture and backed up. "Hey, man, your door was open!"

Maynard positioned himself in the doorway to the room he'd come out of. A big man, he was able to block much of the room from Cole's view. "What do you want?"

"I heard about your wedding. Just wondered why I wasn't invited."

Maynard's little pig eyes narrowed craftily. "I know you. You're a cop."

"I used to be, but that was years ago. Tell me about your bride. I hear she's beautiful."

Maynard relaxed a fraction, turning his head toward the interior of the room. Cole stepped to the side, making an effort to peer into the room, but Sam caught the movement and shifted his body to again block Cole's view. "Whaddaya looking at?"

"Depends. What are you hiding in there?" Cole wasn't really sure he wanted to see what form Maynard's latest perversion had taken, but the man's reluctance to allow him into the room made him determined to get in there.

"None of your business," Maynard snarled. "Get out. I got rights."

"Is that any way to talk? I thought I was invited to the wedding. I just came by to drink a toast. What do you say we tip a couple of beers?"

Sam perked up at the mention of alcohol. He cast one final look into the room, then moved forward, out of the way.

Cole only had a couple of seconds to look, but that was all he needed. Even from that distance, he could see that the walls were covered with pictures…pictures clipped from the newspaper, photocopies of those pictures, pictures taken with a camera of a television newscast, photocopies and enlargements of those pictures…all of Mary.

MARY NEEDED something to do while Cole was visiting with Sam Maynard, something to take her mind off what might be happening across town.

Cole had told her to move things from drawers or shove them aside so she could put away her clothes. Sleeping in Billy's room had seemed enough of an invasion of the boy's privacy; she hated to do more, but it was ridiculous for her clothes to lie on the floor. With a silent apology to Billy, she opened the top drawer of the dresser to see slightly disorderly rows of small underwear and socks as well as a rubber snake, a couple of crayons, a chocolate bar and a slingshot.

The carelessly stored toys, still waiting to be reclaimed, brought home to her the loss of a precious child. From the bits and pieces she remembered of her own childhood, it had been a happy one. It didn't seem fair that this boy had been able to enjoy so little of his.

She closed the drawer, understanding why Cole had been unable to move anything in the two rooms.

The middle drawer was packed with blue jeans, shorts and T-shirts.

When she pulled on the bottom drawer, it opened only a few inches then stuck.

Reaching inside, she found a book wedged between the two drawers. Fumbling, Mary determined that the book was taped in place. What had Billy considered so private that he had gone to so much trouble to hide?

After twisting and tugging for a couple of moments, she was finally able to extricate it and open the drawer.

The book proved to be a journal with the top cover askew and damaged. Apparently over time the tape had loosened enough to allow the book to partially fall and wedge when she'd tried to open the drawer. The damage of her tugging and the tape was sufficient that the first page was exposed.

"Cole and I are married!" The writing flowed across the page, spidery and fluid, filled with loops and flourishes. "I never knew I could feel so wonderful and so safe."

Angela's journal.

Though she knew it was ridiculous, Mary's heart clenched at the thought of Cole belonging to the woman who'd written those words, of Cole making that woman feel wonderful and safe, just the way he'd made her feel.

At the same time, she felt guilty for reading what Cole's wife had written. Nothing in Angela's journal was any of her business.

The book weighed heavy in her hands and guilt seared through her chest. She settled the cover into place as best as she could, and slipped it under the two small sweaters that were the only items in the bottom drawer.

None of her business.

Yet as she put her few clothes in beside the sweaters, she fancied the journal vibrated with the intensity of the secrets that lay between its pages.

"Cole and I are married!" Angela had written. "I never knew I could feel so wonderful and so safe."

But that was only the first page. If Angela had remained happy and filled her journal with similar ecstatic comments, why had she felt it necessary to hide that journal in Billy's room?

Was there more to Cole's anguish than just an automobile accident that had taken his beloved family?

Did the book she'd found contain a key to his ordeal, to the darkness he'd beaten back and the steel that encased his heart? If she knew those secrets, could she then figure out a way to deal with her own problems, to conquer the formless, all-pervading fears that ruled her life, or would she find something in those pages that would worsen her fears?

Mary closed the drawer and stared at it for a long moment before she went downstairs and out onto the patio. She felt the need to get as far away as possible from that journal, from her desire to take it out and search for the secrets to Cole Grayson.

Chapter Seven

When Cole returned home and unlocked the front door, he found the alarm had been deactivated. What the hell?

The minute he stepped inside, he knew the house was empty. Not only was the silence total, but he had no sensation of Mary's soft essence. Had something happened? Had Mary's fears been real after all? Had the person who'd splashed blood on her dress found her and taken her away with him?

Telling himself he was being ridiculous, he ran upstairs to find Billy's room empty. She was nowhere on the first level, either, not in the living room, dining room or kitchen. Then through the window in the patio door, he saw Mary sitting in a white wrought-iron chair, her back to him as she faced the woods.

He walked out, and she whirled around with a start, then smiled, and for a moment, all he saw was that smile.

The woods that encircled his house kept the temperature cool and the air fresh, and Mary, wearing a pair of denim shorts and a faded denim blouse, looked as cool and fresh as the woods. For that moment, all he wanted was to pull up a chair and sit beside her, share a glass of wine as they enjoyed the serenity. For that one moment, he forgot all the turmoil in the world outside, all the turmoil behind Mary's sculpted features and haunting eyes.

"Hi," she said. "Did you talk to that man?" Her tense words brought him back to the reality of the situation.

"Yeah, I talked to Sam Maynard." He took a seat, turning his chair to face her, grateful for the small table between them even as he wished it away. He had to fight the urge to take her into his arms, to somehow protect her from the story he had to tell.

As he recounted his visit to Maynard's house, she sat rigidly straight, her hands clasping the chair arms, her eyes widening with horror.

"The creep had saved every newspaper article and taken photographs from the television news stories about you then had enlargements and photocopies made."

"Did you get them away from him and tear them up?" She shuddered. "I don't want him looking at my pictures. I feel like he's looking at me."

Cole didn't like the idea any better than she did. He reached across the table and laid a hand on her slim forearm. "I had to choose between rushing into that room and ripping up as many pictures as I could before Sam came after me and we got into a fight, or doing what I could to make sure he'd leave you alone."

He'd almost opted for the former, his anger bursting from a seething volcano inside his gut when he'd seen those pictures, that sick invasion of Mary's innocence. He'd wanted to provoke a fight with the big man, wanted to feel one fist connect with and break the beaked nose while the other swung upward into Maynard's jaw and crunched that bone, too. He'd wanted to beat the man to a bloody pulp, erase any thoughts of Mary from that vile mind.

But he'd called on his years of training as a police officer and made himself do the logical thing. He'd grabbed the collar of Maynard's filthy shirt and pulled him close, so close he could smell the man's fetid breath, then warned him what would happen if he didn't destroy his collection and forget about the woman in those photographs.

"So my pictures are still on his wall."

Cole's heart clenched at the disgust in her tone. She thought he'd failed her, and in a way he supposed he had. "I told him to get rid of them. I warned him that he'd answer to me if I found out he kept any of them or if he bothered you in any way."

She shook her head slowly, her gaze slightly unfocused, and Cole wasn't sure if she was seeing the past or the present. "He won't listen. He doesn't believe you."

He squeezed her arm reassuringly as he remembered the fear in Maynard's beady eyes. "He believed me. He knows I'm a former cop, and he's scared of me. After twelve years on the force and three as a PI, I know how to read people. Trust me, Sam Maynard did not take my warning lightly."

She studied him in silence, her gaze coming back into focus then flicking over his face as if searching for the truth…as if he had any truth to give her. Finally she nodded, and the total trust in her eyes hit him broadside.

He had frightened Maynard. He was certain of that. However, Cole wasn't convinced that Sam had done anything other than collect Mary's pictures. When he'd told Sam to forget about Mary, the man hadn't known who Cole was talking about. None of the news stories had used that name. If they'd used a name at all, it had been Jane Doe. Maynard had referred to her as *Grace,* his mother's first name. Apparently he'd seen the same resemblance Cole had noted in the old photograph and thought his mother had returned...in a wedding gown, so she must be his bride.

Cole had not corrected him regarding the name, but had made a mental note that the person who'd called for Mary at the hotel couldn't have been Sam since that caller had specifically asked for Mary Jackson.

But he didn't mention to her his doubts about Maynard being her tormentor. If she thought the problem had been resolved, perhaps she would stop worrying about every phone call and every shadow. He very much wanted to earn the trust he saw in her gaze, to be able to give her that peace and freedom from fear, to see her eyes clear and happy like the springtime sky, instead of haunted and fearful with the ghost of winter. If her tormentor was flesh and blood, Cole could protect her. If her tormentor lived in her mind, all he could do was try to give her a small break from the fear.

"Would you like a glass of wine?" he asked. "I could sure use one right now."

"Yes," she said. "Thank you."

While Cole went back inside to get the wine, Mary tried to digest the news of his visit with Sam Maynard. She believed Cole when he said he'd warned and frightened the man. She believed that Sam would think twice before trying to contact her.

So why was that hard, cold core of fear still lying in her gut like a chunk of lead?

At first she'd felt safe in Cole's house. But then the

rabbit and the phone call had stolen that feeling of security. Only when Cole was beside her did the fear diminish, and even then it didn't vanish completely.

She had to discover what she was running from. Only then could she overcome it.

The door behind her opened, and she heard Cole return.

He walked around in front of her and offered her a glass of wine, blood-red wine.

The darkness started to close around her, like curtains on a stage, but she shoved it back and stared at the crimson liquid, at the transparency that suddenly overlay the scene around her...a tall blond man who smiled as he offered her a glass of wine, a blur of people seated at tables in a restaurant, five women at her table, friends who were making an effort to pull her out of the depression she'd fallen into after her parents' deaths.

Her parents' deaths?

"Oh!" Mary lifted a hand to her mouth to stop the sobs that threatened to burst forth.

Cole was there instantly, kneeling in front of her, concern creasing his forehead, his strong hands on her shoulders, steadying her and pushing back the intruding, unwelcome memories. "What is it, Mary? What's wrong?"

She wanted to collapse against him, feel his arms around her, cry against his broad chest until the sea of tears that swelled inside her was drained, but the desire had a déjà vu quality to it, as if she'd already done that and regretted it. With the blond man? He'd seemed to be friendly, smiling as he approached her.

"I—" She swallowed back the sob that tried to climb out of her throat as she spoke. "I was at a restaurant with friends. They insisted I go out. They were concerned because I'd been so depressed after my parents—after my parents died.'' She bit her lip and resolved not to cry even though the tears were already overflowing her eyes. ''I'm sorry. It feels like it just happened, like I just now got the news.''

''You don't have to apologize.'' His arms tightened around her as if to pull her closer. Her position in the chair made that difficult, and she resisted the urge to lean into him. Much as she wanted to be in Cole's arms, she wanted to be there for a reason other than his sympathy.

She nodded, and blotted the tears from her eyes with her fingertips. ''It hasn't been long since they died. Less than a year.'' The painful details washed over her. ''It was carbon monoxide poisoning from their old gas furnace. I tried to get them to buy a new one. I offered to pay for it. I even gave them a carbon monoxide detector, but they didn't use it. They didn't use the smoke detector I gave them either. Dad was so certain nothing could happen to harm any of us as long as he was there, and he swore he'd always be there for us.''

Cole touched the corners of her eyes with his rough fingertips, gently smoothing away more tears. ''Sounds like a wonderful family.''

She nodded. ''They were. I feel completely lost without them.''

''Do you remember any more details about them?''

She shook her head. ''Just how much it hurt when I heard.''

''Go with that thought. Where were you when you got the news?''

''At home. In my apartment. Getting dressed for work. I can hear the phone ringing, see myself picking it up…'' Again she shook her head. ''That's all. I don't know where I live or where I work or who I am.''

''It's okay.'' He stroked her arm, his touch both soothing and electrically charged. ''You've taken another step, and we have another clue. If your parents lived in a small town around here, odds are their deaths would make the local newspaper. I'll see if I can find something on that.'' He moved back to sit in his chair again then handed her the glass he'd brought out earlier.

For a few moments they sipped the wine in silence, the only sounds those of nature…birds, insects, the breezes rustling the leaves overhead. The setting offered comfort as Mary struggled to deal with this new knowledge about her parents, knowledge she didn't want but had to accept.

''I like being out here,'' she finally said. ''The trees and everything. I always enjoyed going home to the country, getting out of my apartment.''

''Tell me some more details about the place where you grew up.''

She concentrated, trying to bring her childhood out of the darkness. Finally she shook her head. ''I can't.''

''Did you have a garden?''

To her surprise, his simple question produced a vivid image in her mind. ''Yes, we did. A large one with all sorts of vegetables. Mom spent most of the summer canning and freezing. I used to love to dig for the first new potatoes. It was like a treasure hunt. And I'd eat the cherry tomatoes straight off the vine. Mom would fuss at me about washing them, but that wouldn't have been the same. I liked to stand among the plants, barefoot, of course, pluck off the tomatoes, juicy and warm from the sun, and pop them into my mouth.'' She smiled. ''I did that as an adult, too.''

He returned her smile. ''Barefoot?''

''Sure. Barefoot so I could feel the warm earth and the cool grass. I always sunburned so easily, I had to wear sunscreen, hats, long sleeves, slacks.''

''Your skin is very fair.''

''I know. I wanted to be tan like the other kids. But even when I got out without the sunscreen or the protective clothing, all I ever turned was red. One time we drove down to Galveston and I had a wonderful time playing in the sand and the ocean, but the next day I was the color of those tomatoes. Did you go to Galveston when you were a child?''

''No.''

Mary had been focused inward toward her past, the rediscovery of her youth, but the emptiness in Cole's single-word reply brought her attention back to his face. His expression was shuttered, his square jaw more rigid than usual, his gaze turned toward the trees with their solidity of greens and browns that matched his eyes.

''Are your parents still alive?'' she asked.

''No.'' He repeated the word in the same tone.

''When did they die?'' Cole didn't answer immediately, and she waited, wondering if this would be another of his secrets. Though he'd invited her into his home readily enough, had even held her in his arms and kissed her, he seemed determined never to let her past the shield he'd erected around himself.

''My dad died when I was sixteen, my mom five years later.''

''Did you have brothers and sisters?''

''Three sisters.''

"And you're the oldest." It was a statement, not a question. He would have been the oldest.

He looked at her then. "Yeah. I'm the oldest."

"You took care of your mother and sisters." It was another statement. Considering the way he'd taken her into his home and was trying to help her, she didn't doubt for a single minute that the sixteen-year-old Cole had been just as intent on caring for his family.

"I tried." He swirled the remaining crimson wine in his glass before tilting it to his lips.

"I can't imagine that you'd ever fail at anything."

He gave her a taut smile. "Whose life are we trying to recall, yours or mine?"

"Maybe both." Mary surprised herself with the boldness of her reply, her presumptuousness in suggesting Cole, a man so obviously in control, might need to dredge up the details of his life in the same way she needed to find the details of her own.

For a long moment, Cole said nothing, though the closed expression in his eyes and the tense set of his jaw spoke volumes, and Mary wished she could take back her words.

But then he nodded. "I guess that's fair. You're staying in the same house with me, but you don't know anything about me."

She grinned. "We started out even on that score."

"Yeah, we did, didn't we?"

"And now you know that I grew up in the country, went barefoot and ate tomatoes straight off the vine. Your turn."

"I grew up in the city, not too far from here, as a matter of fact. At least, that's where we started out. We moved quite a bit after my father died. He was a cop.

Killed in the line of duty. My mother never got over it.''

"Did you?"

He shrugged. "Do you ever get over losing somebody you love?"

She shook her head, tears threatening again. "No, I don't think so."

"But you learn to live with the loss. You learn to get on with your life because you don't have any other choice."

Sure you do, she thought. *You can always take the coward's way out and forget everything.*

"What happened after your father died?"

"My mother had to go to work. She'd never worked before, so she didn't have any marketable skills. She went through a series of low-paying jobs while I worked part-time at the local service station. We survived. I joined the police force as soon as I could and things got better, but it was too late. My mother wasn't strong. She died within the year, and you know the rest."

You know the rest?

She wanted to protest that she certainly did not, wanted to ask why his wife had hidden her journal in her son's room, whether the sadness that lived at the back of his eyes came solely from the combined losses of first his parents, then his wife and stepson, or whether something else had happened.

Even if she'd had the temerity to ask any of those things, she wouldn't have had a chance. He stood and picked up their empty glasses. "We need to check out the label on your dress while the stores are still open."

Checking out that dress was the last thing she wanted to do, but Cole was right. That was what they needed to do. It was the next logical step in reclaiming the rest of her life, and right now she wasn't at all sure she wanted to do that, either.

But she was more than ever determined that she wasn't going to let Cole see that fear. She wasn't going to let him see how much she needed his caretaking. She didn't like the image of herself in such a needy role.

She must have lost her spirit with her parents' death. That must be why the memory of the blond man bringing her a glass of wine at a restaurant, an act of kindness, a flattering act, was not a good memory.

She squared her shoulders and preceded Cole into the house.

THE PLASTIC BAG containing the wedding gown still lay on the coffee table in the living room where Cole had put it when they'd returned earlier. The dress was folded so the stained area was hidden. Nothing showed but satin and white lace. Yet it was still a repugnant sight.

Mary knew she didn't have the courage to pick it up and was grateful when Cole did. He carried it into his office, the only lived-in room she'd seen so far in the house. Shoving aside a pile of papers, he laid the bag on his desk. While he opened it and took out the dress, Mary perched on the opposite corner of the desk and braced herself by gripping the edges tightly with both hands.

Time seemed to drag as he lifted it, and the dress unfolded as if in slow motion. Mary willed herself to remember choosing the elaborate style, trying it on, checking her reflection in a mirror. Surely those were happy memories.

Nothing came. The dark stain on the front intruded on every image she attempted to conjure up, blotting out everything else.

Cole cast her a quick glance, then, apparently deciding she was holding up adequately, checked the back neckline of the dress. "Where do they put the label on these things?"

Mary licked her dry lips. "Try the zipper." She knew she ought to help him, to hold the garment while he unzipped it, but she couldn't move, couldn't possibly bring herself to touch it.

"Here it is," he said, and read a name that meant nothing to her. "We need a picture. Probably not a good idea to take the real thing with that stain into stores to ask if anybody recognizes it."

"A picture's not going to be much better, is it?"

"I'll clean it up on the computer."

With only a couple of phone calls, Cole was able to determine that the dress was expensive and would only be sold by a few of the most prestigious bridal shops in the city.

"Well," he said, turning in his chair to face her, "we've finally got a solid lead. First I'll try to pull up something on the death of your parents, but even if I don't find that, with this information on your wedding gown, by tomorrow at the latest, Mary Jackson, you may know who you really are."

"Good," she made herself say. "Thank you for everything." But the words were as lacking in enthusiasm as her heart was. In spite of her brave resolutions, she was still fearful of what horrors she would discover buried in her own mind. Besides that, she was equally fearful of leaving Cole Grayson, who seemed to have as many secrets as she did but had found the strength to face his, and who had already passed on to her so much of that strength.

And if she were completely honest with herself, she'd have to admit that she was reluctant to leave him for another reason. No matter how much or how little of her life she could recall, she was certain she'd always remember the feel of his lips on hers, of his body pressed against hers, even the warmth of his hand as he'd stroked her arm on the patio. The touch had been soothing and comforting, but no matter the context, there was always something magnetic and sensual in Cole's touch.

As if he could read her thoughts, his gaze on her grew warm, green sparks spreading through the brown.

Abruptly he looked away from her, turning his chair to face the desk again, pulling open the top drawer and reaching inside. "You won't want to forget this."

His expression was controlled, though the green had not disappeared from his gaze as he extended a hand to her, the diamond ring lying in the center of his palm.

The sparkling stone and his words hung between them like snow-covered mountains.

You won't want to forget this, he'd said. Because she would be leaving soon. Because the ring represented a commitment on her part even though she couldn't remember that commitment. Because the ring still recalled a terror she couldn't face.

She lifted a hand that seemed heavy and detached from her body. As if manipulating a mechanical crane in a toy display at a carnival, she directed her hand in jerky movements as she reached for the ring. Her fingers shook as she lifted it from his palm, and try as she might, she couldn't hold on. The ring slipped to the floor, landing noiselessly on the carpet at her feet.

She stooped to retrieve it at the same time Cole slid from his chair and reached for it. Their hands brushed, and she pulled back. He picked up the ring with one hand, placed it in her palm and folded her fingers over it, then took her arm and helped her to rise.

But when they were standing, he didn't release her arm and she made no move to back away. She wasn't sure she could if she tried. They were too close, the attraction between them too strong. The metal and stone of the ring were cold in her hand, but the cold couldn't survive against the fire in Cole's eyes and the heat his nearness sent surging through her body.

Slowly his hand slipped from her arm to her back, trailing sparks along the way, and she felt her breath quicken. She could be leaving tomorrow, returning to a world she didn't remember and wasn't sure she wanted, a fiancé she couldn't remember and wasn't sure she wanted. Surely whatever fates might be couldn't begrudge her one more kiss from Cole's lips, one more moment of passion in his arms.

A voice somewhere in the back of her mind asked if she'd have the strength to pull away this time, as she'd done when he'd kissed her last night. If she didn't, would they stop with a kiss? Did she want to stop with a kiss?

Cole's gaze dropped to her mouth as he traced one finger around her lips. Every nerve in her body focused on his touch, and her lips parted with a sigh as the tantalizing sensations spread throughout her body like ripples from an earthquake.

She lifted her arms to wrap around him, to enclose him in her center of being, but as her fingers spread to touch his neck, something slipped from her hand, something cold and hard that fell between them. Cole jerked backward, the ring effectively separating them.

This time she stood frozen as he bent to retrieve the diamond and place it in her palm again.

"I'm sorry," he said. "I just can't seem to control myself around you."

"I'm not sure I want you to." Mary amazed herself at the boldness of her comment. She looked down at the ring in the palm of her hand. "I know I should feel some sort of loyalty to…somebody. But it's hard when I can't remember." *It's hard when your touch sets me on fire and makes me feel alive.*

"But you will remember." He turned away from her and took his seat at the computer. "I'll see if I can find anything about carbon monoxide deaths around here this year. You're going to have your past back soon. And when you do, if you're in any sort of danger, I promise to keep you safe."

He promised to keep her safe. Maybe that was what she needed, but right now it certainly wasn't what she wanted from him. It was a good thing Cole had more of a sense of duty to the man who'd given her that ring than she did.

It didn't feel like a good thing, though. Being in Cole's arms, anticipating his kiss…that felt like a good thing.

The rest of the evening stretched before her, turgid with the unreleased tension between the two of them. Then tomorrow they'd probably discover the origin of her wedding dress. Tonight was likely the last night she'd spend under the same roof as Cole Grayson. She didn't anticipate sleeping soundly.

MARY AWOKE from the nightmare with a start, disoriented, heart pounding, and for a moment she wasn't sure where she was.

Cole's house. Billy's bedroom.

In her dream she'd been running through a maze of buildings, her steps hampered by the hated bridal gown, the breath of her pursuer hot on her neck.

A dream or a memory?

It didn't matter. For the moment, she was safe in Cole's house, safe from everything except her own emotions, her desire for a man she shouldn't desire even if she didn't have a fiancé waiting somewhere.

And she might not. He could have been killed, his murderer the one who'd pursued her between the buildings in her dream.

Red digits on the Batman clock beside the bed showed the time as 2:14. She rolled over to try to go back to sleep.

A sound came from the window, and the terror of the dream washed over her again.

A tree branch scraping the glass. That's all it was.

She lay there, listening, knowing sleep was impossible with her heart racing, fear pouring through her veins.

The sound came again, a single tap on the glass.

She didn't recall that the tree was close enough for the branches to reach the window, though perhaps if the wind was blowing...

She forced herself to get out of bed, to confront her fears and back them down, to look out the window.

The wind wasn't blowing. The tree branches were still. A full moon lit the sky and shone off the white wrought iron of the chairs and table on the patio. The night was quiet and serene.

Then movement caught her eye, and her gaze focused on something emerging from behind a tree, something that could only have come directly from her nightmare...a man with no face, his torso covered in blood, arms lifted toward her as if inviting her into his grisly embrace.

Chapter Eight

Mary whirled away from the window, away from the gruesome sight. Heart pounding in fear, she raced across the room to the door, but then caught herself before she could turn the knob.

Where was she going?

To Cole, of course. To his strong arms, to beg him to keep her safe.

No.

She would not again put herself in the position of seeing pity and sympathy in Cole's dark eyes.

Standing immobile, her fingers frozen around the knob, unable to leave the room but terrified to stay, she could almost feel the hot breath of the creature on her neck. The scent of roses seemed to permeate the air, choking her. The room was almost as bright as day with the full moon, but the edges began to darken, urging her away from the things she couldn't face.

No! She wasn't going to run anymore.

Drawing in a deep though shaky breath, Mary pried her fingers from the knob and forced herself to walk back across to the window. Perhaps what she'd seen had only been an unusual configuration of a tree highlighted by the moon shadows, with her fear supplying the rest of the details.

Outside her window, moonlight shimmered on the peaceful scene, illuminating the trees and grounds with no hint of the nightmare vision.

Had she imagined the whole thing?

It was possible, she supposed, then rejected the idea. She *had* seen someone out there. The creature had moved, had stepped from behind a tree and opened his arms to her.

But the woods surrounding Cole's backyard spread before her in their nighttime tranquillity. Whatever had been there was gone. She should close the curtains, go back to bed and forget the whole thing.

Try to forget the whole thing.

No way could she do that. The adrenaline of fear flooded her body, the fight-or-flight response to danger, and she was tired of fleeing. Somehow she had to be certain that no one was hiding in those woods, that those arms weren't out there waiting for the chance to grab her. If she couldn't confront her present fears, what possible chance did she have to confront the fears in her past that lurked just out of sight in her mind?

With a final glance at the undisturbed serenity below, she hurried across the room a second time, out the door and down the stairs, through the kitchen to the back door, quickly, before she lost her courage. Her fingers trembled so badly she had to punch in the code for the alarm system twice before getting it right.

Through the window in the door she could see only what she'd seen from upstairs. The patio with the white wrought-iron furniture. A charcoal grill. The woods beyond. Nothing to fear.

She took the dead-bolt key from its hook beside the

refrigerator, out of reach of anyone who might break through the window but easily accessible in case of fire or other emergency.

Nothing to fear, she told her thundering heart.

But there was no point in being foolish. Opening the knife drawer, she selected the longest and sharpest, unlocked the door, straightened her spine and stepped out onto the patio.

The night was still, too still. Where were the crickets and katydids?

Something moved, rustling in the underbrush and sending panic through her body.

Run! Get away! Escape into the darkness!

Fight or flight!

But she couldn't make herself go forward, couldn't leave the patio with the safety of the open door behind her.

"Mary!"

At the sound of a man's voice, she whirled, knife raised, ready to strike, the light from the moon fading as blackness pressed around the edges of her world.

Cole lunged forward, grabbing Mary's wrist to stop the downward arc of the knife with its blade glittering in the moonlight. Her eyes widened in immediate recognition as she relinquished the weapon to him and sagged against him. At least she hadn't fought him.

"What the hell are you doing out here?" he demanded harshly.

Though the night was warm, she shivered and pushed back far enough that she could look up at him. He kept one protective arm around her, however, restraining her from running away, and, he couldn't deny, holding her close to him.

He was barefoot and had taken time only to pull on

a pair of jeans. She wore a short, silky white gown that clung to her breasts and left her long legs bare. The glow of moonlight lay on her soft skin, highlighting the tops of her breasts. Her slim body against his bare chest felt vulnerable and fragile. In her current state, she shouldn't be desirable, but she was.

For a long moment she gazed at him, long enough for him to see that she was lucid though terrified.

"I saw someone," she finally said. "From my bedroom window. I heard a noise and I looked outside and saw...a man."

He reminded himself that it was possible they had had a prowler. It was even possible someone was pursuing her and that person had somehow found his house. "Where was this man?"

"Right over there." She pointed to the wooded area a few yards away. "He came out from behind a tree."

"What did he look like?"

"He didn't have a face."

Cole tensed. As if she sensed his disbelief, she shook her head and explained, "It was like he had a stocking over his face or something. And there was blood. Blood on his chest and stomach." She trembled, and he pulled her closer, wrapping both arms around her.

She felt so incredibly good in his arms, a perfect fit, her head resting on his chest, her fingers entangled in his mat of hair. All he wanted to do was hold her, make the fear go away. But he knew that wasn't possible. He had to voice his skepticism. "You could see it was blood? At night, from that distance, you could see it was blood?"

She lifted her face to meet his gaze unflinchingly. "The moon's very bright. But, no, I can't swear it was blood. It was a dark stain. It looked like blood."

So rational. He wanted to believe her.

"Why didn't you wake me up? Why did you come out here alone?"

She hesitated for a long moment, her gaze drifting toward the woods, no longer meeting his. "I needed to do this myself."

He wasn't sure if it was a good sign or a bad one that she'd taken matters into her own hands. He held her more tightly, and she again tucked her head against his chest. Her delicate floral fragrance filled his senses and her breath was warm on his bare skin. Her hair captured and enhanced the moonlight, and he fought the urge to run his fingers through the silky strands, to know how moonlight felt.

"If you see anything else, please come get me," he said. "If somebody had been out there, you could have been hurt."

Again she pushed away just enough to look up at him. *"If somebody had been out there?* Somebody *was* there. I saw him. And when I came down, everything was quiet, like it is now, like an intruder had disturbed the night creatures the way we have. Then I saw something moving in the bushes."

"Mary, I just meant if somebody had *still* been out there. I didn't say I don't believe you saw something."

"But you don't believe me. Nobody believes me!" She blinked then backed completely out of his arms, and he could tell by the confused expression on her face that she wasn't sure why she'd made the last comment.

"Let's go inside and sit down," he suggested.

She let him lead her into the kitchen where she waited silently while he locked the door and reset the alarm. They started for the living room, and she rubbed her bare arms, then, as if suddenly realizing she wore only the revealing gown, blushed.

"I need to go put on something."

"I've probably got an old shirt in the hall closet. Sit down and I'll get it."

She waited on the far side of the living room until he brought her the shirt. She slipped it on then darted to the window and closed the drapes.

As she curled in one corner of the sofa, her fair skin and pale hair provided a glowing contrast to the dark blue fabric. The shirt covered the gown but left the long length of her legs exposed.

No more than if she'd been wearing a pair of shorts, he reminded himself, but it seemed like a lot more.

He took a seat in the chair, not trusting himself to sit even as close as the other end of the sofa. Wearing his shirt, and with her legs tucked under her, she was just as tempting as she'd been in the revealing gown. What the hell was the matter with him that he couldn't keep his head on straight around this woman? Why did he have such a hard time remembering that she was fragile and breakable and that she was engaged to another man?

Unless it had been that man's blood on her gown.

"That comment was something from my past," she said, and for a moment he didn't know what she was talking about. For a moment the reason they were sitting in his living room in the middle of the night was totally eclipsed by the sight of her. "I'm not getting any real memories with it," she continued. "Just the frustrating feeling of trying very hard to convince people of something and having nobody believe me."

"People you worked with?" He'd been able to elicit

memories before with questions, drawing from her vivid details of her childhood.

"Yes," she said. "I think so." She hesitated, biting her lip. "Everybody. If my parents had been alive, they'd have believed me, but nobody else did."

"What didn't they believe?"

She shook her head slowly, dismay written across her delicate features. "I don't know. I can feel the frustration and the anger, I can see the expressions of disbelief, I can even see the faces of some of the people, but I don't know who they are or what they won't believe or who I am."

Maybe the questioning only worked with happy memories. That would make sense. Nobody wanted to recall the bad times of their lives.

"There was something else strange when I saw the man outside my window. I thought I smelled roses, and I felt suffocated by the scent."

"There are some wild roses around here. Did you have your window open?"

"No, of course not. I'd be too frightened, even on the second floor. I don't think it was a real smell, more like the memory of one."

"Could be there were roses in the area when you had your traumatic experience."

"Which isn't a very helpful clue, is it?" She stood wearily. "We might as well go back to bed."

For one crazy instant his mind skittered around that comment, imagining she was inviting him to her bed. Of course, she wasn't. His hormones were just spilling over because of the way she looked standing there in his shirt, the way she'd felt in his arms on the patio.

"You go on. I'll be up in a minute." No point in standing and letting her see how he'd interpreted her innocent statement, how much he wanted her in his bed.

She nodded and walked toward the stairs. Ignoring the pull of common sense, he watched every movement...the swing of her hips, the sway of her hair, the flash of her legs.

At the foot of the stairs she stopped and turned back to face him, and he felt suddenly guilty, as if she could read his mind.

"Why did you get out of bed?" she asked. "Your bedroom is on the opposite side of the house, so you couldn't have heard the noises I did. What woke you?"

Her words took him back to that instant when he'd awakened, knowing someone was walking around in the house. He couldn't have said what sound he'd heard, if any. Maybe it was only the vibrations. Living with Angela, his senses had become so sharply attuned for that sort of thing, he hadn't questioned those senses. "The stairs creaked when you walked down them," he lied. They might have.

"You were sleeping at the far end of the hall. You must have excellent hearing."

"Yes, I do." He'd been forced to develop it, and once again it had stood him in good stead. But nothing he had done or could have done was enough to save Angela, and the ache returned with full force. He'd just kept Mary from rushing into the woods in the middle of the night with a butcher knife, but that was a temporary fix. He hadn't changed the final outcome.

"Would you check on that man tomorrow, the man who had my pictures on his walls?"

"Sam? Yeah, sure." He was surprised by the exultant feeling that washed over him at the thought that Sam Maynard might have tracked him down, ignored his warning and tried to peek inside Mary's window. That would mean she really had seen somebody, that she wasn't imagining the whole thing, that the threat to her was tangible and real, something he could fight.

"Yeah," he repeated. "I'll check on Sam, and if he was out there last night, I can promise you, when I'm through with him, he won't be back."

She smiled. "Thank you."

His gaze followed her slim legs as she climbed the stairs until she disappeared from his sight. Then he rose and went into the kitchen to get a beer.

Mary Jackson was messing with his head big-time.

She was engaged, not available for spending the night in his bed. But even beyond that, she'd just admitted to him that she'd had emotional problems before the amnesia. She'd been depressed over her parents' death, and she'd tried to convince her friends of something they didn't believe. He understood only too well how those friends must have felt, wanting to help her yet unable to.

Well, unless he could find a tangible, living, breathing enemy, he couldn't help her, either. All he could do was become as frustrated as they had, beat his head against a brick wall and end up hating himself for his failings.

But apparently that wasn't going to stop him from trying. He'd visit Sam tomorrow and, in spite of knowing he shouldn't, he'd be hoping Sam would confess to spying on Mary tonight. Hell, if he did, Cole would probably be so pleased, he wouldn't even beat the lousy pervert to a bloody pulp.

"OF COURSE they didn't sell me that dress," Mary said with a sigh as they left the third bridal boutique the next day. "I can't even imagine myself shopping in a place like that. My family didn't have that kind of money, and I sure didn't make it teaching school."

Cole grabbed her arm and whirled her around. The midday sun glared down, but even his squinting against it didn't detract from the huge smile on his face. "What did you just say?"

"I said my family—oh!" She hugged him impulsively in her excitement…and wished she could go on hugging him. His body felt so big and strong and secure, just as it had last night when he'd held her on the patio.

She backed out of his embrace reluctantly. "I teach school! Little kids. Grade school." She fought the impulse to hug him again because she wanted to celebrate the excitement and because it felt so good to hug him. But this was neither the time nor the place…and she wasn't sure either of those would ever come.

"I can see their faces," she said, concentrating on the memory, "the whole room of them. Of course, they'll be different faces next year, but I'll see my kids around the school in their other classes, and they always come back to talk to me."

Cole watched her expectantly, but the images had stopped.

"What's the name of the school?"

She shook her head and turned away. "I don't know. It's like all the other memories. My brain filters out the details." Effectively keeping her from discovering her identity, keeping the secrets of her past hidden.

Cole draped an arm around her shoulders, and she reveled in the touch. "That's okay. You're making progress. I haven't given up trying to find something about the death of your parents, we still have two more shops to visit about the dress and now we have another clue. I'll get a list of all the grade-school teachers in the area, and we'll track down every one of them until we find you.''

"That's a lot of teachers if you include the suburbs. Six grades in every school.''

"We only have to check five grades because you said you'll see them next year in the same school.''

"That's still a lot.''

He squeezed her shoulder. "I've solved cases with smaller leads. Let's get some lunch before we visit the last two shops.''

"And check on Sam Maynard.''

He nodded, his jawline suddenly granite. "I'll check on Sam.''

"And I'm going with you this time.''

He didn't respond. He didn't need to. She knew he wasn't planning on taking her, but she also knew she was going along. How could she be expected to deal with her fears if she couldn't face the enemy?

They stopped at a fast-food place for a burger, then drove on to the next expensive bridal boutique. As he'd done before, Cole repeated his fabricated story that they were looking for the woman who'd purchased the dress, Mary's twin sister, then flipped his P.I. badge so rapidly the clerks probably thought it was police ID.

But once again the manager shook her head as she scanned the photo Cole had successfully altered to erase all signs of blood.

"Could you check your records, just to be sure somebody else didn't sell it?" Cole asked, as he had at the other shops.

Predictably, the short, dark woman drew herself up haughtily and whipped off her half-frame reading glasses. ''I can assure you, I'd have known if this gown had been purchased through our store, and I'd have remembered the bride-to-be.'' Her glance told Mary the woman shared her belief that neither Mary nor her fictitious sister belonged there.

''I understand,'' Cole said, ''but just for the sake of the forms I have to fill out, could you check anyway?''

With a disgusted look, the woman disappeared into the back room.

Cole picked up a business card from the elegant gold holder on the table that held large books containing pictures of wedding apparel and swatches of fabric. He started to slip the card into the pocket of his sports coat where he'd put the others, but then stopped and studied it, his forehead creasing in thought.

Mary reached for a card to see what he found so interesting, but before she could look at it, the woman returned.

''We have never sold that particular style from this shop,'' she assured them with a dismissive smile.

''Your card indicates you have other shops,'' Cole said. ''In San Antonio and Houston.''

''That's correct.'' Her tone suggested the matter couldn't possibly be of any interest to them.

''And these other shops carry the same dresses?''

''We all order from the same designers.''

''Could you check to see if the Houston store sold this style recently?''

The woman sighed, but returned to the back room.

''You think I went to Houston to buy a wedding dress?'' Mary whispered the moment the manager was gone.

''Maybe,'' Cole said. ''Remember when we went through the Galleria Mall and you said it was familiar and not familiar at the same time? Well, there's a Galleria in Houston. Maybe you're from the Houston area and that's why nobody has seen your picture and come forward to tell us who you are. Maybe that's why I haven't been able to find anything about the death of your parents in this area. Does Houston ring any bells? Call up any images?''

Mary shook her head. ''Big city. Hot and humid.''

Cole shrugged. ''Things every Texan knows. Still, it's worth a shot.''

''What would I be doing up here if I live in Houston? It's four hours away.''

''Forty-five minutes by plane. Maybe your wedding's going to be here. Maybe your fiancé or his family lives here. Maybe he flew you up in his private jet. You said you didn't have enough money to shop in these places, but obviously somebody did, and I'm betting on the guy who gave you that ring with a stone big enough to throw in the World Series.''

Mary could feel the tension mounting inside her again, tightening her chest and sending anxiety surges along every nerve in her body. ''Maybe I don't want to marry him,'' she blurted. ''Maybe that's what this is all about.''

Cole looked at her for a long moment, but she couldn't read what was going on behind his dark eyes. ''Prewedding amnesia? I don't think I've heard of that one before.''

Neither of them mentioned the blood on her gown. They didn't have to. They both knew there was more to her problem than a reluctance to get married.

She was relieved to see the manager return from the back room and end that topic of conversation.

''Our Houston store did sell a dress of that design

recently. It was delivered to the customer two weeks ago.''

Mary's heart clenched.

''What was the customer's name?'' Cole asked.

''I can't give out that information.''

''I understand. Thanks anyway.''

Mary almost sagged with relief as they walked out of the store. ''Since we didn't get a name, I guess that means this is a dead end.'' She knew she should be upset rather than relieved. Obviously she was still running from her past, glad of any delay in facing it.

''Not at all. Now that I know where the information is, I'll get it. In this day and age, if you have the resources, you can find out anything you want to know. By this time tomorrow, we'll know who bought your wedding dress.''

The afternoon was hot, and passing cars gusted the heated air directly against them as Mary stood on the sidewalk looking into Cole's eyes. Even if she was terrified at the idea of facing her past, Cole should be jubilant. But he wasn't. His gaze was shuttered and noncommittal, dark with no hint of green. She had no idea what lay behind it. Was he, too, worried about what they would find hidden in the dark corners of her mind?

They were halfway home before Mary remembered Cole's promise to check on Sam Maynard.

''After I get you home,'' he said when she reminded him.

''No. I'm going with you.''

''Why would you want to see this creep? He's a disgusting specimen.''

''To know if he's the same man I saw last night.''

''You said that man had something over his face.''

"I might be able to tell by his size or the way he moves." She turned sideways in the seat and appealed to his stony profile. "It's the same reason I had to go outside by myself last night. If I don't learn to confront my fears, how am I ever going to confront my past and get my memory back?"

Cole didn't answer, but he turned at the next block and headed toward the part of town where Sam Maynard lived.

"That was foolish, what you did last night," he said. "You could have been hurt."

"I had a knife."

Cole snorted. "It took me less than a second to get that knife away from you."

"I let you take it!" she protested. "I'd have fought a stranger." She knew that for a certainty. Last night when she'd stood on the patio and heard someone behind her, in the instant before she realized it was Cole, she'd been prepared to plunge the knife into an attacker.

She'd lain awake the rest of the night wondering if she had already done exactly that, if she had stabbed someone.

"It wouldn't have mattered if I'd been a stranger. Anybody bigger and stronger than you could have taken the knife as fast as I did."

That wasn't what she needed to hear. It didn't help in her struggle to gain confidence, to battle back the terrors that remained just out of sight in her mind. "Then get me a gun."

His startled gaze darted from the road to her then back again. "A gun?"

"To protect myself. An attacker couldn't get a gun from me if I shot him before he got too close."

Cole whipped around a corner. "What do you know about using a gun?"

"Well, I know you can be a lot farther away from someone when you shoot him than when you stab him."

"Have you ever shot a gun?"

"I don't know." She folded her hands in her lap and sighed. The fading bruises on her wrists mocked her notion that she could somehow defend herself. "I don't remember. Probably not."

"Then you don't need to have one."

It was just as well. If she had stabbed someone, she certainly didn't need to have a gun.

On the other hand, if she'd seen someone stabbed, if she'd witnessed a murder, she needed to have some way to protect herself.

Cole drove in silence for the next few minutes, until he pulled up in front of a ramshackle house where Mary would have sworn nobody could possibly live.

"He's home," Cole said. "That's his car."

Mary reached for her door handle, but Cole stopped her. "Stay here."

"How am I supposed to see him if I do that?"

"I'll bring him out on the porch. That's as close as you need to be, about the same distance as from your window to the woods. You can see him but he doesn't need to see you." He opened the door and started to get out, but then hesitated with one foot on the asphalt and looked at her. "I'll show you some self-defense techniques tonight," he said. "A few basics you can use to protect yourself in case you should ever need to."

She smiled. "Thank you." He hadn't admitted she'd

really seen somebody last night, but he had admitted she might need to protect herself.

She watched him as he strode up the cracked walk and across the wooden porch. Every line of his body, every movement spoke confidence. He was going into a house to confront a man who was certainly unbalanced and might be dangerously unstable, yet he showed no signs of fear. She envied him that courage. No matter how hard she tried, how many self-defense techniques he could show her, even if she had a gun, she doubted that she would ever be that brave.

Maybe it was necessary to be tempered in whatever fire had scorched Cole's life. Of course, it was likely she'd experienced horror in her life, too, but the difference was that he'd faced his demons even though it was obvious they still tormented him. She'd run away, both mentally and physically. She hadn't possessed his internal fortitude. Nevertheless, she was resolved that she would, in the future, confront her demons no matter how terrified she might be while doing it.

Cole had only been in the house a few minutes when he came out again, his expression grim as he strode down the walk toward the car. He looked at her once as he opened the door, then looked away.

"Wasn't he there?" she asked.

He didn't answer. Instead, he opened the glove box, retrieved his cell phone and punched in a number.

"Pete Townley… Then find him, damn it! This is an emergency."

A chill darted down her spine. "Cole, what's the matter? What's going on?"

"Sam's dead."

"Dead? How?"

"Looks like a suicide."

''Now we'll never know for sure if that was him last night.''

Cole didn't reply and didn't meet her eyes. About that time Pete apparently came to the phone, and Cole related the facts of the incident to him.

No response to her last comment and no eye contact so she could see what he was thinking. Mary sensed that Cole was hiding something from her, something that indicated he knew Sam Maynard hadn't been the man outside her window last night.

If it wasn't Sam, then who?

Chapter Nine

It was early evening before they started back home, and Mary's self-defense education had risen to the top of Cole's priority list. The circumstances of Sam Maynard's death, along with the possibility that they could discover who'd purchased the dress tomorrow and she'd be gone from his life, lent urgency to the need to teach her to defend herself.

Even if they didn't find the purchaser of the wedding gown, Cole had no doubt Mary would soon recover her memory. The fact that she'd reminded him of his offer to teach her self-defense, that she felt capable of defending herself, told him how far she'd come.

He hadn't answered her question about knowing whether Sam had been outside her window last night, electing to let her find whatever feeling of safety she could from the possibility that her tormentor was dead. However, though he was no expert, he'd seen enough bodies to make an educated guess as to how long Sam Maynard had been dead, and that guess would be at least twenty-four hours. Whoever Mary had or hadn't seen from her window last night, Sam Maynard had already been dead at the time.

The circumstances of his death muddied the waters

even more. On the surface, it looked like a suicide. Cole had found him sitting on one end of the ratty sofa in his living room, a half-empty water glass of cheap red wine, a single pill and a suicide note on the floor next to him. The note had been typed on an old typewriter left in the house by Sam's mother.

If I can't have Mary, I don't want to live anymore.

Open and shut.

Except it wasn't that simple. Sam had never been known to be suicidal nor had he ever been involved in drugs. Still, those issues probably wouldn't have raised any red flags if not for the note. The correct spelling and punctuation and the lack of typos, even for such a short, simple sentence, were beyond Sam's capabilities, but the major problem with the note was Sam's reference to *Mary.* He'd been adamant the day before that her name was *Grace.*

However, Cole wasn't about to tell Mary that the man had most likely been murdered. She'd complied with his request to wait in the car while he talked to Pete and the other officers in the house, so at the moment she knew none of the details except what he'd told her.

If Sam Maynard had been murdered, the fact that Mary's name had been mentioned in the suicide note indicated the incident somehow involved her. Further evidence in that direction was the fact that all her pictures had vanished from his house.

Though Pete wasn't convinced that Sam's death was linked to Mary, that it was anything other than the suicide it seemed to be, Cole's gut told him it was.

If he'd followed his gut reaction that cold, foggy night three years ago, Angela and Billy might not have died.

He pulled into his garage and, as he and Mary walked to the front door, he found himself scrutinizing the area carefully for signs of an intruder. He was becoming as paranoid as Mary. But perhaps with reason. He made a mental note to replace the burned-out bulb in the porch light.

Once they were inside, she watched him quietly as he reset the alarm. The drapes in the living room were open, and he noticed that she glanced in that direction as if she'd like to close them, hesitated then moved on into the room. She hadn't overcome her fears, but she was fighting them.

He'd been attracted to her since that first evening, an attraction he had a tough time fighting with her here in his house. Her strong will and determination to overcome a faceless, nameless terror only increased that attraction.

She sank into one corner of the sofa, drawing her knees to her chest and wrapping her arms around them. She looked so fragile and vulnerable and so incredibly beautiful, he wanted to go to her, pull her into his arms and comfort her.

Instead, he sat on the other end.

"It's okay to be upset," he said, trying to reassure her. "The first time I ever saw a dead body, I had nightmares for weeks."

She hugged her knees tightly. "I guess you got used to that sort of thing when you were a police officer."

He ached to move down the sofa, pull her to him and soothe away her pain.

And if that was all he wanted to do, he'd do it. The truth was, he wanted to feel her body next to his, her lips on his, her skin beneath his hands. He wanted to soothe her pain, drown it, along with his, in the velvety depths of passion.

"You don't really get used to it," he said in answer to her question. "You just learn how to shut it out."

She considered that for a moment. "In a way, you've done the same thing I've done."

"Well, yeah. I never thought of it like that before, but I guess it is sort of similar, just not to the same extreme."

She gave him a faint smile. "I suppose total amnesia is carrying it to extremes. Apparently that was the only way I could deal with it. I'm not as strong as you. I know it's kind of trendy to complain about having a dysfunctional childhood, but I think mine must have been too good. It didn't prepare me for real life."

"Too good? I didn't know that was possible."

She shifted a little, getting more comfortable, more relaxed, and a sad smile tilted her lips. "My parents were wonderful. I still can only recall glimpses of that part of my life, but I think it was so wonderful, I never wanted to leave, never completely left, in fact. My dad helped me make all decisions, everything from choosing an apartment or buying a car to making friends. He was a very wise man, and I wouldn't have dreamed of doing anything without talking to him. My mother always encouraged me in everything I did, always on my side, always there for me. I guess I never really learned how to be strong, to stand on my own. When I lost them, I lost my entire support system."

"But you had a job, teaching school, and apparently you enjoyed your work."

"Yes, I did. I loved working with the children, and I had friends. It's just that I'd always leaned on my parents. My father told me what to do, and my mother gave her approval. A pretty good system. If they'd been around, I don't think—'' She shook her head and sighed. "I don't know. I still can't quite see what happened."

"Somewhere along the line you met the man you're engaged to," he encouraged.

She frowned. "He sat down next to me at a concert."

Cole felt a jolt to his entire system. The man Mary planned to spend the rest of her life with had suddenly become real. "So you met your fiancé at a concert."

She looked confused for a moment. "My fiancé? I don't know. I just had an image of a man coming up to sit next to me at a concert, but that's not where I met him. He was at that restaurant I mentioned, the first time I went out after my parents' death. He brought me a glass of wine."

"What did this guy look like?"

"Tall, blond hair, tan, well-dressed."

"The type who'd buy you that gaudy diamond?"

Mary glanced up sharply, and Cole realized his tone had betrayed what he was feeling…jealousy. He resented this unknown man in Mary's past for going to the concert with her, for holding and kissing her when he presented her with the diamond engagement ring.

"I suppose it's possible," she said. "But thinking about him makes me feel suffocated. I get the feeling he's very confident, the salesman type who doesn't let up until he gets what he wants. Perhaps that's why I ran away. Maybe I let him push me into agreeing to marry him and then didn't have the strength to tell him I'd changed my mind."

Cole cringed at the sense of relief that comment brought. He was getting pretty damn proprietary over a woman he didn't really know, a woman who was engaged, a woman who needed all kinds of things, including someone strong and competent to take care of her. She'd just admitted as much in talking about her father. Without someone to guide her, she was lost, and he didn't do so hot in the field of helping people.

He needed to get control of his hormones. So what if they'd kissed? He'd kissed a lot of women.

But he couldn't recall a single detail of the lips of any of those women, while he could recall every detail of Mary's lips, of the full, sensuous way they looked, of the warm, soft feel of them, the way they'd moved against his. He could recall, in far too vivid detail, how the curves of her body had fit in his arms.

Suddenly even the far end of the sofa was too near Mary. He got up, distancing himself from her, and went to lean on the fireplace mantel.

"Maybe you needed somebody like that man when you were feeling so vulnerable after your parents' death, somebody you could lean on."

Or someone she thought she could lean on. Where was her fiancé when that gown got bloody? Where was he when she ran away from whatever caused her amnesia? Cole had been berating himself for not being able to take care of Mary, but this guy hadn't done such a great job of it, either.

Which had nothing to do with anything, Cole reminded himself irritably. Who Mary chose to marry was none of his business. Once he tracked down the purchaser of her wedding dress, his role in her life was over. He'd be off the hook, no longer responsible for her.

To his consternation, that thought brought a sense of loss, not one of relief. He'd become accustomed to seeing her around his house, to her scent in his car, to the accidental touches when they passed in the hall or as he helped her clean up the kitchen…to the heated desire she sparked in him just by her nearness.

Damn! He really needed to get his head on straight!

"I always wanted a marriage like my parents had," Mary said. "They were so close, they were like one person. I don't recall them ever fighting about anything."

He folded his arms and gazed into the distance, into another time. "Mine fought, but mostly over Dad's job. Mom worried about him, and with good reason. But when she wasn't worrying, she was always laughing and happy until he died. All that laughter died along with my dad. She just lost the will to live. She wasn't strong enough to go on without him." And Cole hadn't been competent enough to help her.

Mary had to resist the urge to go to Cole, to wrap her arms around him and comfort him even though she knew the urge was ridiculous. He looked so big and powerful and sturdy leaning against the fireplace, one blue-jeaned leg positioned on the hearth, his arms crossed over his wide chest. He was the last man in the world who needed comforting.

Or at least he was the last one who'd accept it.

But she was beginning to understand him better. Now she knew where some of the sadness and torment in his eyes came from. Even as a teenager, he'd probably had that same concern for others, that same determination to care for people that he'd shown with her. He'd undoubtedly taken seriously his obligation to care for his family and been distressed that he couldn't help his mother. Then the double loss of Angela and Billy had compounded his devastation.

"You can't save people from themselves," she said, swinging her legs off the sofa and sitting upright, facing him squarely.

His eyes darkened, all traces of green disappearing, and he seemed to be retreating into himself again.

"Where are your sisters now?" she asked hastily in an effort to divert him from whatever she'd said wrong, to keep him with her.

"Tammy's married with one kid and living in Chicago. Glenda and Alyse, the twins, are both still here in Dallas. They're starting their own business, a gift shop. They're all doing good."

"Do you see them often?"

He stooped to pick up a piece of lint from the carpet then tossed it into the fireplace. "They have their own lives and so do I. But, yeah, we stay in touch, get together for holidays. I hear every time that niece of mine spits up or cuts a tooth. And every time one of the twins falls in love again, which is pretty often, I have to meet the guy."

As he spoke of his sisters and niece, Cole's rugged features actually relaxed into something approaching a smile. Perhaps this was the right time to bring up the people Mary had wondered about since she'd walked into Cole's house.

"How did your sisters get along with Angela and Billy?"

That question took care of the smile. He was back to being Mr. Inscrutable. "They got along fine."

Obviously this was going to take a more direct question. "Tell me about Angela and Billy. I feel strange, staying in Billy's room with all his possessions when I never even knew him."

"Billy was a good kid. He was a little shy, but he

was coming out of it. A pretty typical kid, I guess. He liked football and baseball, wanted a dog, hated homework.''

''I saw the baseball things. Did he play on a team?''

''He played at school. He wanted to play football, too. He was a little short for his age. His mother was short, but his father was tall. He'd probably have grown.''

''Angela was short?''

''Barely five feet tall.''

''Dark hair?''

''Yeah. How'd you know that?''

''I saw the picture in the master bedroom.''

''Of course.''

''What was she like?''

''Shy. Billy got that from her.''

He must have loved Angela very much, Mary thought, her heart clenching. Must still love her very much that he could barely talk about her three years after her death. ''I'm sorry. I didn't mean to bring up something painful.''

He shrugged. ''It's in the past. Over and done.''

It wasn't. She could see that in the determined jut of his jaw, in the hollow emptiness behind his eyes, in his inability to talk about her. But at least his losses hadn't shattered him. He was dealing with it. He hadn't broken into a thousand pieces, then shoved the painful pieces completely out of himself. He was a whole person.

''I wish I had your strength,'' she said. ''I wish I could face my past and accept it.''

''You will. You're getting stronger every day.'' His gaze returned to the present, to her, and she glimpsed approval in his eyes.

Even as she drank in the warmth of that approval, she hated that she needed it so much, that she was still unable to stand on her own.

She rose abruptly. "Are you ready to get started on those self-defense techniques you were going to teach me?"

"Yeah, we need to do that."

He moved away from the fireplace and came so close to her, she could smell the clean fragrance of his soap and the masculine scent that belonged to him alone, could feel the electricity that passed from his body to hers.

As he approached and took her arms, for a moment she thought he was going to pull her against him, kiss her, make love to her, satisfy that craving he started in her just by his nearness, that craving that intensified every day with every word he spoke to her, every small detail of himself he permitted her to see.

Of course he wasn't going to do any such thing. He was going to teach her how to defend herself against an attacker. He was simply continuing to take care of her the way he'd taken care of everyone in his birth family and his married family. She could be in danger, and he was trying to help her. That's all. And that was all it should or could be.

She found it hard to imagine wanting another man— the tall blond man from the restaurant and the concert?—but when she regained her memory, she might regain her feelings for the man who'd placed that hated ring on her finger. Unlikely as that felt right now, it was a possibility and should be a barrier to thoughts of kissing Cole.

Should be.

"It wasn't Sam outside the window last night, was

it?'' she asked, redirecting her thoughts and giving voice to her suspicions concerning the danger she might be in.

He hesitated only briefly before replying. ''I don't think so. I'm pretty sure he was already dead by then.''

''I saw someone.'' She paused, holding his gaze. ''Do you believe me?''

''The only thing that matters is that you believe it.''

''*I* believe me,'' she said.

Mary's quiet words had the unexpected ring of confidence, Cole thought. He'd told her the truth when he said she was getting stronger every day. He suspected she'd soon be strong enough to face whatever awaited her in the world she'd chosen to forget. And then she'd be gone from his world.

In the meantime, he'd do what he could to ensure that she'd be able to protect herself just in case.

He ran through some of the basic techniques of self-defense—raking the attacker's eyes with her fingers, knee to groin, half fist to throat, palm heel to nose, kicks or pressure to knee or elbow—techniques that, coupled with the element of surprise, could gain her enough time to get away from an attacker.

She was a quick and energetic learner. There was only one problem. All the demonstrations involved being close to her, holding her body against his, and it was tough to concentrate on anything but the feel of her.

As he wound one arm around her neck and the other around her shoulders, then pulled her backward to him, he knew she must feel his hardness, must know that his ragged breathing didn't come from physical exertion but from the way she affected him.

''Lift one foot,'' he instructed, ''and put the heel

against my knee. It only takes a few pounds of pressure to break a knee when you're pushing from the front. At the very least, you can cause a lot of hurt and use this position to shove off and get away.''

She obediently lifted her foot and pressed the heel gently against his knee, then lowered it. Her bottom pressed against his arousal, and he made no move to release her. Nor did she make any move to get away.

He lowered his arms to wrap them around her abdomen, just under her breasts. Her heart pounded against his hand, strong and fast, matching his own heartbeat. Knowing that she was as aroused as he took away the last of his control.

Burying his face in her hair, he breathed in the fragrance of white flowers, held her close and asked himself if he knew what the hell he was doing.

He had no answer.

He raised his head and lifted her hair, running his fingers through the silky strands. It did feel like moonlight—soft, sleek and gentle. She tilted her head, and he pressed his lips to the throbbing pulse, tasting the sweetness of her skin and hearing the sweetness of her low moan.

"Mary," he said softly against her neck, the single word a question and an entreaty.

Her body tensed and she gasped. "Mary? Who's Mary?"

He released her and took a step backward, trying to clear the fog of desire from his head and figure out what had just happened.

She blinked, lifted a shaky hand to her forehead and laughed nervously. "I can't believe I said that. It just sounded so wrong. I thought you were calling me by another woman's name."

"Okay," he said cautiously, "if your name isn't Mary, what is it?"

"I don't know. It's Mary. For now. I just…I don't know." She lifted her arms in a helpless gesture.

Cole ran a hand through his hair. What the hell was the matter with him? He'd been on the verge of seducing a woman who couldn't even remember who she was or who she was engaged to. Oh, he was taking care of her, all right. About like he'd taken care of his mother and Angela.

A tap sounded at the picture window across the room, and her head jerked in that direction.

"What was that?"

"Nothing. Something hitting the window."

"It's the same sound I heard last night when that man was outside."

Cole went over and looked out into the dusk of the evening. "The wind must have blown an acorn or a pecan against the window." He could see Mary fighting back the fear, and he hated the noise that had caused the return of that fear. But at the same time, it served as a cold shower, reinforcing the wrong of what he'd been about to do.

"It's June. Too early for acorns and pecans to be falling."

She had a point, but he didn't want to increase her fears. "There are always a few left on the trees from last year, but I'll go check just to be sure."

He turned to go, but she caught his arm.

"I'll be okay," he assured her.

"I know." She smiled softly and released his arm. "I just wanted to thank you for checking, for not telling me how silly I'm being."

"Fear is never silly no matter what causes it." And

after Sam's death, Cole wasn't going to dismiss any of Mary's fears no matter how far-fetched they might seem.

He took a heavy-duty flashlight from the hall closet and went out to check.

There were no signs of an intruder, though the signs would have had to be pretty blatant to show up in the rustic setting. The insects and birds were quiet, but that could be from his appearance on the scene. Acorns, pecans, twigs and pebbles littered the ground beneath the window. The noise could have come from a natural source. Probably had.

He lifted his gaze from the ground to see Mary standing in the living room, hugging herself and look-ing toward the window even though, with the light on, he knew she'd see only a dark reflection of the room.

But he could see her quite clearly, and the situation felt strangely erotic.

She bit her lip, drawing one corner into her mouth, and Cole found himself mimicking her action as if he could somehow touch her lips instead of his own.

There were plenty of logical reasons why he shouldn't make love to Mary, but his body didn't know about logic. His body only knew how much he wanted her.

MARY WENT UP to bed early that night, claiming ex-haustion. It was the truth. The self-defense session had been physically tiring, but mostly her exhaustion came from that scorching scene with Cole, his breath in her hair, his lips on her neck, finding sensual spots she hadn't known existed, the hard feel of his arousal that told her he wanted fulfillment as much as she did, and then the frustration of stopping short of that fulfillment.

After Cole came in from checking and finding nothing, they'd eaten a quick dinner. She'd forced down half a sandwich and sat through some television show, though she couldn't say which one, before making her excuses to come up to bed. However, she didn't anticipate sleeping much. Her body was still aroused, still wanting Cole, and she couldn't stop her mind from replaying over and over every detail of their sensual encounter even though such repetitions only increased her frustration.

She closed the bedroom door behind her and flipped on the light.

Angela's journal lay open on her bed.

Cole must have taken it out of the drawer and left it like that. But why?

And *when?* They'd been together all day, and she couldn't recall his coming upstairs after they got home.

For no good reason, she approached the bed cautiously, fearfully.

The journal was open to the first page, except it was a different first page. Angela's exuberant joy at being Cole's wife had been ripped out of the book.

Was this Cole's way of telling her that he knew she'd peeked in the journal?

No, Cole wasn't sneaky. He would have simply confronted her.

So who had put the journal on the bed? Who had torn out that page?

Feeling ridiculous, she checked the closet to see if anyone was hiding there.

Of course no one was. The house was secure. Cole had locked the door and set the alarm system when they left. It had still been set when they came home.

No one could possibly have been in her room except Cole.

But the question still remained, who—and when?

Obviously Cole had even though she hadn't noticed. He had all but refused to talk about Angela. Could this possibly be his way of letting her know about their life together? For whatever reason, apparently he'd torn out that page and left the journal open for her to see.

Unless she'd done it herself, ripped the page from jealousy of another woman's happiness, then blocked that action from her mind the way she'd blocked the rest of her life.

Surely not. The part of herself she did remember would never have done anything like that.

Feeling sick to her stomach, she sank onto the bed and with trembling hands picked up the journal. The exposed page showed a slightly different handwriting, still basically the same as that first spidery note, but shakier, less fluid.

Feeling more than a little guilty, Mary turned a few of the pages and noted that the handwriting soon became unrecognizable as Angela's.

Against her sense of decency, she focused on one of the paragraphs.

Bill has found us! Cole says the alarm system will keep everybody out, but I know Bill too well. I've had to deal with him all these years. Cole hasn't. He doesn't understand!

Bill? Billy's father? Cole had never mentioned Angela's ex-husband other than to say he was tall.

Of course, Cole hadn't told her very much about Angela.

Fascinated and unable to stop herself from invading Angela's privacy, Mary read on and soon deduced that Billy's father was a psychopath. He had tried on several occasions in the past to harm Angela and Billy. Cole had bought the isolated house and put in the alarm system with the sole purpose of protecting his wife and stepson from a maniac.

No wonder Cole didn't want to talk about it!

Had Bill finally murdered his ex-wife and child? Cole had said they'd died in an automobile accident, but maybe it hadn't been an accident.

Cole had still been a police officer then. Had he been unable to protect his family from a murderer? That would explain why he'd left the police force. It might also explain his tortured soul, his inability to go into their rooms, as if their memories would accuse him.

The entries stopped halfway through the book. By that time, Angela's terror was total, her handwriting unrecognizable and almost unreadable.

She had never returned to her son's room to reclaim the journal.

Once again Mary wondered why she'd found it necessary to hide the book in Billy's room, away from Cole. But apparently Cole had known about it.

Unless she herself had been the one to rip out the page and leave it on the bed.

That's crazy.

The sentence screamed at her from the black void of her life, filling her with a dark sense of dread.

Had someone said that to her? Even if they had, it was the kind of thing that might be said in a fit of anger. It didn't necessarily mean that she was mentally unbalanced.

Did it?

She tucked the journal under Billy's sweaters again, getting it out of her sight in the hope that she could get the disturbing thoughts it had brought with it out of her head.

As she unbuttoned her blouse to get ready for bed, she suddenly felt exposed.

The bedroom window, like the other windows in Cole's secluded house, had drapes that were never closed. Tonight, she closed them.

She'd been right about sleep not coming easily. Between thoughts of Cole, of needing him beside her, fears about her own mental stability and questions about Angela's journal, Mary found herself wide awake as the digital clock flashed away the hours.

"You hurt me and even though I forgive you, you must pay."

Mary sat bolt upright at the sound of the whispered words, her heart pounding so hard it threatened to burst out of her rib cage. Someone was in her room!

Her fingers trembled so badly she almost knocked over the bedside lamp as she fumbled with the switch. The light finally flashed on, blinding her momentarily.

It revealed an empty room.

"I'm here. I'll always be here."

She gasped as the voice came again. She couldn't tell where it was coming from. It seemed to be all around her.

She was hearing voices.

The mystery of the journal with its missing page hit her again, along with the memory of someone telling her she was crazy.

"You betrayed me, and you'll have to be punished."

She burrowed under the covers, pulling the pillow over her head, trying desperately to get away from this latest horror. With her heart pounding so loudly, surely she wouldn't be able to hear it again.

Stupid! she berated herself. If the voices were all in her head, hiding under the covers wouldn't help, nor would her heartbeat drown them out.

She threw back the covers and sat up.

Damn it, she hadn't imagined the voice! It was real.

For the second night in a row, she forced herself to get out of bed and confront her fears. As her feet hit the floor, she fully expected some monster to reach from under the bed and grab her ankles.

"Eventually you'll learn."

The voice came from everywhere.

She grabbed Billy's bat and moved cautiously to the closet. She'd checked it before. It had held nothing but Billy's clothes.

Nevertheless, cold fear gripped her as she swung the door open.

Nothing.

"Those who truly love will always forgive no matter how grave the sin."

That sounded somehow familiar, but the terror that gripped her refused to let her think, to remember where she'd heard it before.

She had to open the curtains and look out the window.

This time was harder than the first. She turned off the light with trembling fingers then walked on wooden legs over to the window and stood for a long moment, cold sweat breaking out on her forehead.

Do it! she ordered herself. But her hands remained at her sides. If she opened those curtains, would she see the monster from the night before just outside her window, hovering in midair, whispering from a mouth he didn't have?

''Soon we'll be together.''

She jumped as the voice came again.

Cole would open those curtains without a second thought. He'd jerk them back and confront whatever might be out there no matter what the horror he had to face.

She needed to be as strong as he was, to face her terrors.

Her hands seemed to weigh a ton each as she lifted them and clutched the fabric in fingers that were stiff and no longer wanted to obey her commands.

Mustering every ounce of courage she had, she pulled the curtains aside, and for a moment she saw and felt nothing, retreating again to the safe darkness of her mind. It was so enticing to return there, to get away from all the bad things, all the frightening things, forget the mysterious voice tonight, the bloody man beckoning to her last night, her parents' deaths…but not Cole. She didn't want to forget Cole.

Her focus shifted and once again she saw a peaceful, tranquil scene stretching before her, moonlight illuminating everything.

There was no one outside her window.

No one in the closet.

No one but her in the room.

What had she heard?

Nothing.

You're crazy!

She ran her tongue over her dry lips. Was she mentally unbalanced…enough to hurt someone? Did that explain the blood on her wedding gown?

She didn't want to remember yet suddenly she knew

that she had to. She could no longer live like this, terrified of the unknown, hearing voices—had she really
heard the whispers or were they merely echoes of her
past trying to reach her? Though she listened intently,
she heard nothing else.

Mary turned away from the window. She had to get
the dress and the ring, look at them, hold them in her
hands, accept them into her life and make them give
up their memories to her.

Since she wasn't likely to sleep anymore tonight in
this room, she might as well go downstairs and get it
over with now.

Chapter Ten

Cole awoke with a start. Whether as a result of good hearing or a sixth sense developed from living with Angela, he knew with certainty that Mary was downstairs again.

Damn! Had she seen someone else from her window? Would he again find her wielding a knife and chasing a murderer or a phantom? He wasn't sure which would be worse.

She'd made so much progress, he tended to forget—wanted to forget?—how fragile she still was.

He yanked on his jeans and hurried downstairs, his gut clenched in a knot.

At the bottom of the stairs, he saw light coming from his office. His heart thudded against his ribs as he charged around the corner and into the room.

She whirled to face him, her eyes wide and startled. She held the stained wedding gown in one hand, and in the other the diamond ring.

"You remember." Cole heard the sadness in his own voice and realized with dismay how much he feared the return of her memories…the return of her pending marriage to another man.

"No," she said. "I thought maybe this dress and

this ring would spark something, but they haven't so far.''

Cole was astonished and dismayed at the relief that washed over him. She didn't remember. Not yet, anyway. At this moment in time, there was no other man in her life.

No other?

Yeah, no other. No one but him. He felt that in his heart and read it in her eyes.

She looked away, putting the ring and the dress on the desk behind her. The fact that she'd been able to come down by herself and confront those articles told him a lot about how far she'd come. This time— maybe—he had been able to help. Though, he realized, the difference was not in what he'd done but in how Mary had reacted. At some point along the way, she'd started trying to help herself. Neither Angela nor his mother had been able to do that. No matter how hard he'd tried, he hadn't been able to do everything for them.

Maybe no one could have.

The thought brought him a sense of peace he'd never known.

''I didn't mean to wake you,'' Mary said, still avoiding his gaze. Her breasts, covered only by the skimpy fabric of the gown she'd worn the night before, rose and fell with her quickening breaths. ''I should have waited until morning. I'm sorry.''

''It's okay.'' He'd be happy to be awakened anytime he could see her dressed like that. Hell, anytime he could see her no matter what she was wearing. In blue jeans and a cotton shirt she set his hormones flowing. But in that wisp of a gown she made it hard to remember all the reasons he shouldn't make love to her.

She lifted her head, returning her gaze to his, her eyes smoky with desire. "I couldn't sleep," she said, and he wasn't sure if she was continuing their conversation about her being up in the middle of the night or whether she was admitting that she'd been thinking about this attraction that surged so strongly between them.

Not that the words mattered. The husky tone in her voice and the look in her eyes broke down any defenses he might have had left.

He took a step toward her, closing the distance between them, and she moved into his arms, lifting her mouth for his kiss. With a groan, he pulled her to him, surrendering all common sense to the passion she aroused in him. There were at least a thousand reasons why they shouldn't be doing this, but at the moment he couldn't recall a single one. At the moment, his entire world consisted of the feel of Mary filling his arms, her lips moving on his, the tip of her tongue darting and teasing, her heart beating in time with his in a wild, savage rhythm.

All the tension and restraint of sleeping under the same roof with her, of being so near her, of all the "accidental" touches that set him on fire, exploded in an overwhelming surge of desire.

He caressed the soft skin of her back, then slid his hands over the thin fabric of the gown to her slim waist and along the curve of her hips, obsessed with the need to touch and claim every inch of her. She was slender and delicate, but tonight she didn't feel fragile. Tonight the length of her as she pressed against him was solid and real and he'd never wanted any woman so much in his life.

Cupping her bottom in both hands, he pressed her

more tightly to him even as he knew the only way he could ever be close enough to her was to be inside her, a part of her.

He trailed kisses along her throat, down to the creamy roundness of her breasts. Last night he'd thought the moonlight on her shoulders was the most beautiful thing he'd ever seen, but her translucent skin was just as beautiful in the harsh glare of the overhead light.

His fingers feeling clumsy and overgrown, he traced the curve of her breasts. When he slid his hand inside her gown, her nipple pebbled immediately at his touch, and her eyes half closed as her head tilted slightly back while she sucked in a quick breath. Her reactions almost pushed him over the edge. He couldn't stand another moment of the exquisite torture.

His lips moved to hers again, and she responded with an intensity he would never have believed possible from someone who'd seemed so timid. Tonight she was no longer timid. Tonight she'd held the ring and the dress voluntarily and without fear. Tonight her body pressed against his with the same urgent need he felt, and he could barely restrain himself from pushing her backward onto the desk, ripping off the flimsy gown and burying himself in her.

He forced himself to pull away, then traced his fingers along her cheek, his gaze searching hers.

"Mary," he whispered, "are you sure?"

"I'm sure." There was no uncertainty in her words or her gaze. It was the only answer he needed to any lingering doubts or questions he might have had.

He scooped her slight weight into his arms and carried her up the stairs, to his bed.

Her moonlight hair fanned out on his pillowcase and

her porcelain skin was creamy against the serviceable white sheets. He feasted his eyes for a moment, then reached to turn off the lamp.

She laid a hand on his. "No. I don't want any more darkness.

He smiled. "Good. I wasn't through looking. I want to see every expression as I make love to you."

Having actually voiced the words, he could wait no longer. Unzipping his jeans, he slid them off, then joined her in bed, his lips again claiming hers.

Mary couldn't remember if she'd had other lovers, but she knew with a certainty that none had ever made her feel the way Cole made her feel, that no other lips had ever kissed her so wonderfully, every movement matching hers in perfect synchronization. His touch brought every nerve in her body to tingling, fiery awareness.

Her arms wrapped around the solidity of him, holding him to her, reveling in the feel of him...the muscles in his back and neck that rippled beneath her hands when he moved, the width of his chest and the coarse mat of hair on that chest...the solid male reality of him. She could feel the hardness of his arousal against her thigh and marveled that she could have caused that reaction in him.

When he slid aside the straps of her gown, cupped her breasts and took one nipple between those magical lips, electricity shot through her and she arched upward with a low moan. He sucked gently, and she was suddenly certain she would burst into flames at any second, completely consumed by her desire for him.

As their bodies tangled together, every spot he touched turned to an erotic zone. She drank in the smell of him...soap and an indefinable scent that belonged only to him and that she would recognize blindfolded. In his embrace she felt strong and sheltered, free to give of herself completely, every inch of her suddenly, wonderfully alive.

When finally he poised between her thighs, she reached down brazenly to guide him into her.

He was steel sheathed in silk, and she gasped at the incredible sensation of his smooth hardness moving inside her.

He stopped, his forehead creased with concern. "Are you okay?"

She smiled. "I'm more than okay."

He grinned and resumed the tantalizing movements. "Yeah, you sure are."

She arched to meet him, responding from a primitive place inside her that needed no memory to tell her how to react. He'd said he wanted to see her every expression, but it was she who watched him as they moved together. She wanted to experience and wallow in every sensation, every look, every sound, every feeling, wanted them imprinted on her memory so strongly they could never leave her.

When he opened his eyes and focused on her, for that moment she felt not only their bodies but their souls blending. She was a part of him and he of her, and then the world exploded in a burst of fireworks that centered at their joining but spread through all of her from the tips of her toes to the top of her head.

Cole groaned, and she could feel him pulsating inside her, joining her explosion of sensations.

He collapsed on top of her, and for a few moments, she shivered in delight at the aftershocks.

When the ability to think returned, she felt certain if the room had been dark, she would have been able to see sparks flying from her skin during the crescendo of their lovemaking.

Cole rolled over and turned out the light then pulled her to him, spoon-fashion. "That was wonderful," he said softly, his mouth moving on her hair. "*You* are wonderful."

"So were you. That was the most incredible experience of my life."

He parted her hair and kissed the back of her neck. "But you can't remember the rest of your life," he teased gently. "How do you know you haven't had much more incredible experiences?"

"Because I could never have forgotten something so amazing. Besides, if it had been any more incredible, I don't think the top of my head would have stayed on."

"I'm not sure mine did." He held her closer, his breath warm on her neck.

Cole's body curled around hers felt so warm and right. Tonight, she knew, she would have no nightmares, hear no voices.

At the memory of those voices, she tensed. How could she offer her body to Cole and not be honest with him? She had to tell him. Even more importantly, she had to tell him about reading the journal.

"Cole," she said, her voice cracking the delicious, velvety silence that engulfed them, "are you awake?"

"Barely."

"I need to tell you something."

"I'm listening." His muted, sleepy voice was the embodiment of satisfaction, and she wanted to give in to the lure to join him there, to forget about the diary and fall asleep in his arms.

But she couldn't. "I found Angela's journal."

"Angela's journal? What are you talking about?"

He sounded surprised. If he hadn't known about the book and hadn't left it open on her bed, who had?

"The one she kept hidden in Billy's dresser drawer."

"I didn't know she kept a journal. Did you read it?"

So he hadn't known. That meant the only person who could have left that book on her bed was her. No intruder could possibly have gotten past Cole's alarm system. "I didn't intend to read it. I know I shouldn't have. But, yes, I did."

"It's okay. I should have told you the whole story before."

"You mean about her ex-husband?"

He sighed. "What did she say about him? That he was stalking her?"

"Yes. He sounds like a psychopath."

"I'd better tell you the story from the beginning." He rolled onto his back, away from her, taking his body warmth and the warmth of their union.

She turned toward him and found him gazing upward at the ceiling. He seemed somehow much farther away than the actual few inches. "I met Angela when I was on the police force. She called in one night complaining about a prowler that she thought was her ex-husband."

Mary shivered in the darkness, feeling and identifying with Angela's fear of someone she couldn't see.

"Said he'd been harassing her," Cole continued in an emotionless monotone. "Pete was my partner then, and he and I checked the entire neighborhood thoroughly but didn't find anything. That's pretty typical when something like that happens. The prowler leaves before we get there." He hesitated, and Mary sensed that he didn't feel emotionless at all, that his emotions were so intense he couldn't release them, couldn't allow them into his words or he'd be swept away by them.

"I'll never forget the way Angela looked when we told her we'd done all we could and that we had to leave. I felt so sorry for her. She was tiny and helpless and scared. Billy was four then, and he was clinging to his mother, just as terrified as she was. I made it a point to stop by periodically after that and see if things were all right." He shifted, rearranging the pillow beneath his head.

"Sometimes Angela was fine, but sometimes she told me horrible stories about the things her ex-husband was doing to her and had done before their divorce. She said she'd moved from Tulsa to Dallas to get away from him, but he wouldn't leave her alone, that he came down every few days to harass her, that he was stalking her. I believed her. I'd been a cop long enough to know that psychos will do whatever it takes to get their kicks, even make a five-hour trip on a regular basis."

I believed her? The words and the way he spoke them caught Mary's attention. Was he suggesting there was a reason not to believe Angela?

"I was there one evening when he came to pick up Billy for visitation. Billy didn't really want to go with him, but his dad was insistent in a quiet but firm way. I figured he was on his best behavior because of me. He's a big guy, bigger than I am, and I was furious at him for what I took to be bullying his own son. I wanted to shove my fist in his face, punch him out, show him what it felt like to be on the receiving end. I didn't, of course. I was polite but I let him know that

I was a cop and that I was taking care of Angela and Billy. He gave me a funny look, and, at the time, I thought it was because I had him worried.''

He turned his head on the pillow then and looked at her. In the moonlight she could see the bone-deep sadness that had drawn her to him from the first, that intimate knowledge of the depths of pain.

''That night was when I decided to marry Angela. In a way, I guess I wanted to do for her what I hadn't been able to do for my mother, rescue her, take care of her. If I was Angela's husband, I'd have the right to talk to her ex, to beat him to a pulp if he bothered her. I'd be around all the time to be sure he didn't hurt either one of them. I can't really say I was ever in love with Angela, but I cared for her and Billy. I didn't want anything to happen to them. So we got married.''

He'd never really loved Angela. He'd only wanted to take care of her. On one hand, Mary felt a tiny thrill of pleasure at that knowledge, but at the same time she reminded herself that Cole was taking care of her, too. Nothing more.

Cole looked away, returning his gaze to the ceiling and laying his arm across his forehead as if to completely block her out of the next part of the story. ''It wasn't long before I realized that her fears were groundless. She'd hear somebody outside or even in the other room when I didn't hear a thing. I finally went to Tulsa and confronted her ex. We had a long talk. He's a nice guy, and he showed me proof that he only came to Dallas once a month to visit his son. He said she started getting paranoid right after Billy was born.''

''But,'' Mary protested, ''what about all those things she wrote in her diary?''

''Fantasies. Delusions. After my talk with Bill, I

tried to get her to see a psychiatrist, get help. She refused. In fact, that seemed to upset her even more.

"So I did everything I could to make her feel safe. I bought this house where it would be virtually impossible for anyone to find us. I put in the best alarm system I could find. When Bill came for his visitation with Billy, I arranged to meet him in a restaurant on the other side of town so he didn't have any idea where we lived. I thought surely she'd realize she was in no danger. But she never did.

"Every shadow was a threat. Every hang-up phone call, instead of being a wrong number, was somebody verifying that she was home. No matter how hard I tried to reassure her, no matter what I did, she was terrified."

Every shadow was a threat. Every hang-up phone call was somebody verifying that she was home. No matter how hard I tried to reassure her, no matter what I did, she was terrified.

It sounded eerily like her own situation, only she was worse than Angela had been. She heard voices, saw a man with no face, forgot her own past, blocked the action of tearing a page out of Angela's journal.

He stopped talking, as if the story had ended, but Mary had to hear the rest of it. "What happened the night she died? After reading the journal, I thought her ex must have killed them, but apparently I was wrong about that."

"Yeah, you were wrong about that." Cole sat up on the side of the bed and stared out the window. "It was my fault."

Finally she knew the source of the torment that held Cole in its unforgiving clutch. In those four words she heard the wellspring of the anguish she'd seen in his eyes and felt in his soul.

"Your fault?" she asked.

"I didn't believe her."

"But I thought you said there was no danger, that she was having delusions. That certainly wasn't your fault."

"She was having delusions but she was still in danger. She called me on my cell phone one night when Pete and I were on a stakeout. We were waiting for a flesh-and-blood bad guy, and I thought at the time it was more important. But Angela was running from bad guys who were worse, ones she couldn't get away from, the ones inside her own head."

"You said her death was an accident."

"*Accident* was a poor choice of words. Two vehicles collided, but it wasn't really an accident. When I didn't come home, she put Billy in the car and left. I have no idea where she was going. I'm not sure she knew. She was probably just trying to get away from the danger. The witnesses say she stopped at a traffic light. An elderly man crossing the street tapped on her window to tell her that she had a low tire. He said she took one look at him, hit the gas and pulled into the intersection in front of a semi. The driver lived, but she and Billy were killed instantly."

Mary could feel the sorrow and guilt emanating from him in waves. "It wasn't your fault," she said in what she knew would be a vain attempt to reassure him.

"I'd heard it all so many times, I ignored my gut reaction that told me she really was in danger that time. I was responsible for her safety, and I failed. If I'd listened, if I'd gone home, she wouldn't have been out in the car. She and Billy would be alive today."

Mary sat up behind him and wrapped her arms around him, pressing her cheek to his broad back, making an effort to comfort him the way he comforted her when she was upset. "Maybe," she said, "or maybe something else would have happened. Cole, Angela was sick. She needed professional help, the kind of help you couldn't give her."

He laid his hand over hers where it rested on his chest, accepting the attempt at comfort if not the comfort itself. "I tried to get her to see a doctor, but she refused. I even considered having her committed for psychiatric observation, but I thought I could take care of her. She was my wife. I had a duty to her, and I failed in that duty."

He turned in her arms and cupped her face in his hands. "Let's don't talk about the past anymore tonight, yours or mine. We can't change the past and we don't know what tomorrow's going to bring. All we have is tonight." He kissed her softly, leaving her lips yearning for more. "I want to make love to you again, Mary. I want to be inside you and around you and completely blot out the rest of the world."

She nodded. "Yes. I want that, too."

She didn't want to think about Angela's story or her own problems. She didn't want to think about tomorrow when she might be proven a killer, or stalked by a killer, when she might be back with a fiancé she couldn't remember.

Though she knew she had been making wedding plans with another man, she found it impossible to believe. How could she make love with Cole, take his body inside hers and scale the heights of intimacy with him, if somewhere in her heart existed love—even a love she couldn't remember—for another man?

That was something she'd have to deal with later, but right now all she wanted was to experience again the ecstasy that came when she joined her body with Cole's.

Their lovemaking this time was slower with more exploration and mutual discovery of each other's bodies, though the pinnacle, when it came, was even more resounding than the first time.

Later as she lay in his arms and felt his breathing deepen and slow when he drifted into sleep, Cole's words continued to echo through her head.

He hadn't loved Angela. He'd felt responsible for her, wanted to take care of her.

That pretty much described the way he'd felt for her when they first met. Responsible for hitting her with his car, responsible for her memory loss, wanting to take care of her, even to the extent of taking her into his home. And she'd accepted that at the time, partly because she'd felt safe with him but partly because she'd been attracted to him and wanted to stay around him no matter what it took.

Tonight they'd met on level ground. Tonight they'd made love, giving and taking in equal portions. That's where she wanted to keep it as long as she could. She was falling in love with Cole Grayson. She knew he would never return that love, certainly not if he knew the truth about her mental condition, about the journal's appearance on her bed or about the voices.

Worse, if he knew, he'd again feel responsible for her. He'd feel sorry for her.

He might never love her, and she might be gone from his life tomorrow if he was able to determine who'd bought the wedding dress. But whatever happened, she wanted him to remember their wonderful lovemaking untainted by the knowledge of her problems.

She would not, could not tell him about the journal's mysterious appearance and missing page or about the voices.

MARY WOKE the next morning with Cole's arms still wrapped around her. She lay perfectly still, savoring the delicious feeling, storing the memory for all the empty mornings that stretched ahead.

Today Cole might find the name of the person who had bought her wedding dress.

Today she might leave Cole Grayson's house forever.

Today Cole might discover that her problems ran as deeply as Angela's had.

But as the first light of morning streaked through the window, Cole's chest and stomach were warm against her back. His arms wrapped around her possessively, his legs tangled with hers and his scent mingled with the essence of their night of lovemaking and filled her senses.

She realized from his quickened breathing that Cole was no longer asleep though he hadn't moved, either. Was he, too, aware of the ephemeral quality of the moment?

Then his hand slid from her abdomen to her breast, and he nuzzled her neck. At his touch, her desire rose.

As they came together in the early light of dawn, their lovemaking reached unexplored, explosive heights though it had an elusive, haunted quality, like maple leaves in autumn that blazed a glorious red even while heavy with the knowledge that the branches would soon be barren and lonely.

Later as Mary lay in his arms, Cole spoke the words that hovered between them. "If I get on it first thing, we can probably know in a few hours who bought that dress."

"That's great," she said. "Thank you."

No! every fiber of her being screamed silently. She didn't want to return to a world she couldn't remember, didn't want to face whatever had been so horrible that she'd forced it to the darkest recesses of her mind, didn't want to remember a man she'd promised to marry. She wanted to stay forever in Cole's arms, feel the early-morning sunshine on her skin, live in the light of the world she'd found.

But of course that was impossible.

MARY WAS SITTING in one corner of Cole's office that afternoon, pretending to read a book while he worked at the computer, when the phone rang. She jumped and the book slid from her lap to the floor.

Cole gave her a guarded look, then glanced at the caller ID. "It's the police department," he said, reaching for the receiver.

That information should have calmed her, but it didn't. Was someone calling to tell them another pervert wanted to take her home with him? Or perhaps even that her real fiancé had finally appeared? She wasn't sure which she dreaded more.

Cole's end of the conversation revealed nothing. The caller was apparently doing all the talking, with Cole grunting or muttering "I see" in acknowledgment.

"We'll be there in an hour, Pete," he said, then hung up and turned to her. "Jessica Doyle. Ring any bells."

She rose slowly as the name slid into its designated slot in her memory. "It's my name, isn't it?"

"Is it?" She thought his eyes begged her to say no, but that was probably only a reflection of her own need, her fear of discovering her identity.

"I think it is." She licked her dry lips and sank back into the chair, afraid her shaky legs would no longer support her. "I know it is but only in the way I know the sun is ninety-three million miles from the earth. It doesn't really have any meaning to me. I don't feel like Jessica Doyle. I still feel like me."

"A man came into the station with one of the posters you and I put up. He claims to know you, and he has a wallet with Jessica Doyle's identification. The address is Houston, and the driver's-license picture looks like you."

She swallowed hard. "The man—?"

"Tall and blond. His name is Geoffrey Sloan."

Though she didn't repeat the name aloud, it echoed round and round through the empty chambers of her mind.

Geoffrey Sloan. The name brought up images of the smiling blond man bringing her a glass of wine, seated beside her at the concert, standing in her doorway holding a huge bouquet of roses, turning from her kitchen sink to greet her with dinner already prepared when she came home from work.

Suddenly cold, she wrapped her arms around herself as a black curtain dropped between her mind and the returning memories. She didn't want to remember Geoffrey. She didn't want him in her life.

She shuddered. That was a strange and terrible way to feel about a man she must have loved once.

Though not so strange, she supposed, after last night. Of course she didn't want Geoffrey. She wanted Cole.

"Your fiancé?" Cole asked.

She nodded, the movement jerky and painful, as if every muscle in her body had tied itself into knots. "I guess."

He came over to stand beside her, almost but not quite touching her. He wouldn't touch her. Not now. Not ever again. "You guess?" he asked, his voice harsh. "Mary, this isn't something you can guess about. You have to be certain."

She clenched her hands into fists, focusing on the pain of her fingernails biting into her palms, anything other than the pain of this moment.

"We dated. I remember that and I remember him being in my apartment when I got home from work, cooking dinner for me. What else do I need to remember to be certain?" Tears hovered in the corners of her eyes, but she blinked them back. She was not going to cry. She was not going to show that final sign of weakness.

He resumed his seat at the computer, turning his back to her. "I'm going to keep checking databases while you pack your things."

Pack your things. Of course. Pack her things and leave Cole's house. She had a name and a fiancé. Cole was no longer responsible for her. She no longer had a place in his life.

She rose stiffly and took one step toward the door then stopped. "The blood," she said. "Where did the blood come from?"

"The kid next door got hit in the nose with a baseball. Caused a hell of a nosebleed." He spun around in the chair, his forehead dark, his expression fierce. "Just because this guy has your ID doesn't mean he's your fiancé. This could be another fruitcake."

"It's okay," she said softly. "I'm sure I know Geoffrey Sloan. You don't have to continue to take care of me.''

He returned to his computer without responding.

She climbed the stairs woodenly to the room where she'd made her temporary home, to the room where Cole's son had once lived. Cole hadn't been able to protect Angela and Billy or his own mother, and he was working extra hard, going to unnecessary lengths, to protect her in an effort to make up for what he considered his failure with his family.

She was Jessica Doyle. She knew that for a fact. And all reason and logic told her that Geoffrey Sloan was her fiancé. She would leave Cole and go with Geoffrey even though the idea terrified her.

She frowned at that thought. There was no reason she should still be terrified of her past. She wasn't a murderer; the blood on her gown had been explained away. She hated herself for such weakness. Obviously she had become far too dependent on Cole, frightened to leave the safety he'd come to represent.

At the top of the stairs, she halted with her hand on the railing and looked back.

It involved more than the safety factor. No matter what Geoffrey had been to her in the past, she didn't love him now and would never be able to…not when she loved Cole with all her being.

Maybe she'd never loved Geoffrey at all. Maybe her relationship with him had been like Cole's with Angela. Maybe he'd wanted to take care of her. She could remember how fragile and lost she'd felt at that restaurant when she'd met Geoffrey. Was she more like Angela than she realized…a frail, mentally ill woman who heard voices and saw menacing figures, a woman a man could only feel pity for?

Was the nameless terror she'd been running from her own mind?

As she took her clothes from the drawer of Billy's dresser and returned them to the shopping bag, she only knew one thing for certain.

She loved Cole Grayson as a man, not as a protector, even though she knew that whatever strength she'd gained had been given to her by him.

Against all reason, she hoped that he'd find another man had purchased the wedding gown and she wouldn't have to leave with Geoffrey Sloan.

Ten minutes later she descended the stairs carrying all the worldly possessions of Mary Jackson.

Cole strode from his office to meet her, his dark gaze shuttered. "Geoffrey Sloan put your wedding gown on his platinum credit card."

Icy fingers wrapped around her heart. "I see."

Cole extended his hand and for one insane moment she thought he was reaching for her, asking her to stay.

But the diamond ring lay on his palm. "You'll probably want to put this on."

The irrational fear that still accompanied everything tangible and intangible from her past life washed over her, but she refused to accept it. The ring was only an object. It couldn't hurt her.

Leaving Cole would hurt. Spending the rest of her life without him was the most frightening terror she could imagine, a terror she had to face.

Numbly she took the ring from him and slid it onto her finger. The metal was cold against her skin.

"Are you ready to go?" he asked.

She nodded, unable to speak the horrible lie. She wasn't ready to go. She would never be ready to leave him.

Was it only yesterday that Cole had told her she was growing stronger every day? She didn't feel strong at all. Her legs were so shaky she could hardly stand as she walked through that door out of his house to return to a life she barely remembered and didn't want.

Chapter Eleven

Geoffrey Sloan was handsome and charming and Cole hated him on sight.

Mary—Jessica—sat stiffly in the chair next to him, across the table from Pete and Geoffrey in the interrogation room Pete had commandeered for this meeting. He could feel the waves of tension emanating from her as she wrapped slim fingers around her cup of vending-machine coffee. One of the posters he'd made up, folded and slightly crumpled, lay in the middle of the table.

"You still don't remember, do you?" Geoffrey asked, his model-perfect features molded into an expression of sympathy and compassion.

"Sort of. Bits and pieces."

Was it Cole's imagination or did Sloan's face go slightly paler under his smooth tan? Was his orthodontist-perfect smile a shade tight? Did he not want her to remember? Was this man hiding something?

"'Bits and pieces' is a start," Sloan said smoothly. "When I saw that poster with your picture and the caption Amnesia Victim, I was frankly worried. That worry increased when I came here and Officer Townley told me the amnesia was total. The fact that you're starting to recover is a good sign.''

Sloan was saying all the right words. Cole told himself that his suspicion came only because he was having a hard time relinquishing Jessica—his Mary—to another man. He'd always known this day would come and thought he was prepared for it.

What he hadn't counted on was the way she'd fit into his arms and his heart so perfectly.

What he hadn't counted on was the feeling of despair that had hit him broadside when the call had come from Pete, when he'd known he was losing her, that he'd never again hold her or make love to her, never again taste the sweetness of her lips or smell her white floral scent.

He knew she still had a lot of problems to overcome and he knew she'd be better off in familiar circumstances. He knew he didn't have the ability to help her. He knew that, once she regained all her memories, she'd also regain her love for Geoffrey Sloan.

He knew all those things, but somehow none of that knowledge eased the ache in his gut or the sense that things were not right.

Pete set a brown leather purse in the middle of the table. ''Check inside,'' he instructed her.

Mary lifted the purse carefully. Obviously she had no sense of it belonging to her.

She took out a slim beige wallet, a gold tube of lipstick, a white comb, three restaurant mints, a couple of pens and a small memo pad. He watched as she opened the memo pad and flipped through the pages...all blank. She opened the wallet and revealed credit cards, as well as her driver's license with the name Jessica Doyle beside a picture that certainly looked like her.

Without a word, she opened the memo pad, took the cap off one of the pens and wrote "Jessica Doyle," then compared it to the signature on the driver's license.

"It's me," she said softly without looking up.

If he'd needed final confirmation, that was certainly it. She was not Mary Jackson, the woman who'd shared his life and his bed. She was Jessica Doyle, a woman who belonged to Geoffrey Sloan.

Sloan scooted his chair back and rose stiffly, smiling down at her. He seemed a little tense, but Cole supposed that was normal under the circumstances. "Of course it's you, Jessica. Will that be sufficient, Officer Townley? Can we go home now?"

"I have a few questions," Cole said, his voice loud in the small room.

Pete's expression was inscrutable. He could have told Cole this was none of his business, but he didn't. So maybe he wasn't quite comfortable with this guy, either.

Sloan shifted his gaze to Cole. "Grayson, right?" he asked. "I understand you've been very kind to my fiancée, but I also understand you're the man who hit her and caused her memory loss. What sort of questions do you have?"

Cole leaned back and crossed his arms, refusing to be intimidated. "I can see you're anxious to be on your way, to be reunited with your lovely fiancée. I'll try to keep this short."

Sloan inclined his head in a half nod.

"So why did it take you so long to get here? Her

picture's been in all the newspapers and on all the television stations.''

"I was in Houston.''

"What was Mary…Jessica…doing in Dallas?''

"The wedding plans were stressful for Jessica. Her parents died in a horrible accident, and she's been… sensitive…since then.'' He looked at her with compassion that bordered on pity and made Cole want to lean across the table, grab the lapels of Sloan's expensive suit with one hand and break his nose with the other.

Jessica ducked her head.

Sensitive? What the hell did Sloan mean by that? Was he saying she was mentally ill?

Maybe she had a few problems, but Mary—*Jessica*—wasn't mentally ill!

"My father has a condo in the Turtle Creek area,'' Sloan continued, "that he uses when he has business up here, so we decided to use it for a couple of weeks to get away. I had to return to Houston to take care of business, but Jessica's a teacher and has the summer off so she stayed here. I was a little concerned when I couldn't reach her by phone, but sometimes she retreats like that. She can be a very private person.''

He smiled down at her with a sympathetic, knowing expression, and Cole clenched his fists, anger and resentment washing over him at another man looking at his Mary that way, talking about her as if he knew her intimately. Which, of course, he did.

Deal with it! Cole ordered himself. Get over the jealousy and deal with giving Mary into the hands of this slimy bastard who must be really a nice guy after all or she wouldn't be engaged to him.

"When I returned this morning,'' the slimy bastard

went on, "I found the door to the condo unlocked and Jessica gone. Still, I wasn't worried until I found her purse. I went next door to ask the neighbors if they knew anything, and their ten-year-old son told me that he'd been hit in the face with a baseball, which resulted in a terrible nosebleed. Since his mother was at the store, he went to Jessica. Jessica was trying on her wedding gown, and when the boy ran up to her, he got blood all over the gown. He said she looked at the blood and started screaming, then ran out of the building."

"That seems like an awful lot of blood for a nose-bleed," Cole interrupted.

"The boy's a hemophiliac. That's why it was so important for him to get immediate attention. Which he did from another neighbor after Jessica ran away." He paused to give Jessica another sympathetic glance and Cole's fists again clenched. No matter how hard he tried, he couldn't like this guy, couldn't feel good about Jessica's going with him.

"Knowing her state of mind," Sloan went on, increasing Cole's disgust, "of course I was frantic until I noticed the poster in the lobby of my building. I came to the station immediately."

"Why didn't your neighbors call the police when she first ran away?"

"They're very conservative, the type who don't want to get involved in anything to do with the police. You know how some people are."

Cole knew only too well how some people were, so there was no reason for him to be suspicious of Sloan's story. Yet he was, probably because he just flat didn't like the man, didn't like the way he looked and sure didn't like the way he talked about Jessica.

But he had to admit that he was prejudiced. Maybe the only reason he didn't like Sloan was because he himself was personally involved with Jessica. Because he was looking for any excuse to stop her from going off with this man.

Sloan hadn't done such a great job of taking care of Jessica. He'd left her alone, hadn't been there when she'd needed him.

Yeah, kind of like the way you left Angela alone, weren't there when she needed you.

He rose from the table abruptly. Sloan took a step backward, as if shoved by Cole's anger. For a moment Cole took great delight in glaring and watching Sloan flinch.

"Well," Cole said, "I'm glad everything worked out. Mary—Jessica—if you ever need me, you know where to find me." He turned and started for the door, trying to escape while he could, before he did something stupid and made a complete fool of himself.

But Jessica stood and placed a restraining hand on his arm.

"Please don't go before I get a chance to thank you for everything you've done." Her gaze held him more surely than her hand.

"You're welcome." He made no further move to leave.

"Geoffrey, Officer Townley, would you excuse us for just a minute?"

"Jessica, I—" Sloan started to protest, but Pete cut him off.

"No problem. We'll be right outside."

As soon as the door closed, Jessica sank into the chair again.

Cole sat down beside her but she kept her gaze focused on the table, away from him.

"Look," he said, "if you don't want to go with that guy, you don't have to. You can stay with me until you get on your feet."

As he spoke the words, he realized how desperately he didn't want her to go. Against all logic and reason, he wanted her to stay with him. Not because he had any illusions that he'd be able to take care of her and not because he felt responsible for her. No, his need to keep her with him was purely selfish. He'd be lost without her.

"Yes. I do have to go with him." She picked up the wallet, closed it and stuck it in the purse.

"Why?" He braced himself to hear that having met Geoffrey, she remembered her love for him.

"I haven't been completely honest with you."

"Not honest with me? What are you talking about?"

"Geoffrey said I'd been *sensitive* since my parents' deaths."

"You mentioned you were depressed. So? Who wouldn't be under the circumstances?"

She returned the rest of the items on the table to the purse before she answered. "Do you remember when I told you about reading Angela's journal?"

"Yeah."

"I read it because I found it lying open on my bed with the first page torn out."

"How did the journal get on your bed? Who tore out a page?"

"I thought at first you'd done it."

"You thought I'd done it? I didn't even know Angela kept a journal."

"I realize that. The only other person in your house was me. I must have done it then forgotten it."

A chill darted down his spine. "More of the amnesia."

"I guess."

"But you're coming out of that. You're regaining your memories. It's just a matter of time."

"There's more."

He waited.

"Last night I heard voices in my room."

He didn't understand what she was saying...or didn't want to understand. "You spent the night in my room."

"Before that. Before I went downstairs."

"You dreamed you heard voices?"

"No. I was awake. I heard whispers, things like, *You hurt me and even though I forgive you, you must pay, you betrayed me, and you'll have to be punished, those who truly love will always forgive no matter how grave the sin.*"

"That last part, isn't that what somebody said to you on the phone? Remember, you answered and that's all whoever it was said before they hung up."

She looked at him, her face pale and drawn, a study in despair. "I thought I'd heard that one before, which means either I imagined it the first time as well as the second, or I remembered it and incorporated it into my delusions."

Delusions. The room was suddenly hot and stuffy, so stuffy he could hardly breathe.

He didn't want to hear that word from her. He didn't want to accept all the implications...that she had as many problems as Angela, that he couldn't help her, either...that he'd failed again and she was lost to him forever. The stakes were higher than before, the loss more devastating since this time he stood to lose not only someone he cared for but a piece of himself.

"What are you trying to say?" he demanded.

She rose and settled the strap of the purse over one shoulder. He shot up beside her and for a long moment she held his gaze unflinchingly. "I don't know what I'm trying to say. I don't know what's going on. I don't know what's wrong with me, but something is."

"And you think by going with that guy, you can find some answers?"

"He's the only link to my past that I've found so far."

"Do you love him?"

She dropped her gaze to the floor and shook her head. "No."

"Are you going to marry him?" He knew he sounded angry and jealous, but he couldn't help it. He *was* angry and jealous.

"I don't think so."

"You don't *think* so? How could you even consider marrying a man you don't love?"

Her head jerked up at the rising tone of his voice. "You married a woman you didn't love," she accused. Though her words seemed unusually quiet after his outburst, they echoed loudly through his mind as she turned and walked out the door and out of his life.

She was right, of course. He hadn't loved Angela, and that, he realized, was the center of his problem. He hadn't loved her enough to listen and believe, to go home when she'd needed him.

He resumed his seat in the hard chair and waited, giving Sloan and Jessica time to get out of the station. He didn't want to see them together.

Pete came in a few minutes later, slid back one of the chairs and straddled it.

"They gone?" Cole asked.

"Yep. You okay?"

"Sure. Why wouldn't I be? Did you check this guy out?"

"Yep. He's legit. His dad's a big wheel in the Houston area, owns a few strip shopping centers, hobnobs with the mayor, the police chief, the judges, all those folks. Son works in the family business and moves in the same circles. He has friends on the police force down there, and they were only too happy to vouch for him."

"Well." Cole slapped the table. "Good. I'm glad to hear that I don't need to worry about Mary. I mean, Jessica."

Pete lifted one eyebrow. "Sloan's friends said he has his hands full with that young lady. Seems this amnesia isn't the first mental problem she's had. Her family died suddenly several months ago, and she went into a deep depression. That's when Sloan met her and, being the nice guy they all say he is, kind of took her under his wing. Next thing they know, Sloan's telling them he's going to marry the woman in spite of what they called her *erratic behavior.*"

Cole scowled. "*Erratic behavior?* What's that supposed to mean?" Hearing voices? Forgetting things she'd done?

"The guy I talked to down there said one day she'd be crazy about Sloan, not want him to leave her apartment, then the next she'd be calling the police and accusing him of stalking her, breaking into her apartment."

"She told me she remembered the guy being in her

apartment, cooking dinner for her." What Pete was telling him only verified all the evidence. Jessica was emotionally unstable and needed someone strong and competent, someone like Geoffrey Sloan, to take care of her. Whether or not Sloan could help her was anybody's guess, but for sure Cole couldn't.

"We got the autopsy results back on Sam Maynard," Pete said. "You were right. Homicide. He died from a drug overdose, but he didn't take it voluntarily unless he figured out how to give himself a shot in the back of the neck and then dispose of the needle after he died."

In the shock of Geoffrey Sloan's appearance and Jessica's disappearance, Cole had momentarily forgotten about Sam's death.

"What about the wine and the pill beside it?"

"The wine was laced with a powder form of the same drug, tetracyanazine, known on the street as Good Time Charley."

"Good Time Charley? Isn't that a happy-time drug?"

"A little has a mellowing effect, makes the person very agreeable and compliant. A lot puts the person to sleep. We're guessing the perp probably spiked the wine with enough to make Sam groggy so the killer could then inject a lethal dose. Takes a lot of Charley to kill somebody, and the stuff has such a bitter taste, it'd be hard to get him to drink that much."

Cole released a low whistle. "Any idea who the perp might be?"

Pete shook his head. "Not so far. No sign of forced entry, which usually means somebody the victim knew and trusted."

"The door was unlocked the day I went over there."

Pete nodded. ''Even the two of them sitting down to have a glass of wine doesn't mean Sam knew the person. Hell, he was so much in his own fantasy world, he could have thought he was having tea with the queen of England.''

''Yeah. This may be a tough case.'' Cole drummed his fingers on the wooden tabletop. ''I guess his death didn't have anything to do with Jessica after all.''

''Apparently not.''

''Well, I'm glad we got her case solved anyway. Got her back with her fiancé.''

''Me, too. I liked her. I'm happy everything turned out good for her.''

''Yeah. Good. The best.'' No matter if letting her leave with Sloan felt like the worst mistake he'd ever made. No matter if it left a ragged hole in the middle of his chest where his heart used to be. No matter if he dreaded going home to an empty house worse than he'd dreaded going to that house after Angela's accident.

Jessica had thought he was so strong. If she only knew how weak he felt right now.

''How ARE YOU DOING, sweetheart?'' Geoffrey steered the big luxury car with one hand while he patted hers with the other. They were moving at a snail's pace, caught in the tail end of rush-hour traffic on Central Expressway.

''Okay,'' she said automatically, then changed her mind about the white lie. ''No, that's not true. I'm not okay. I'm confused and scared.''

''Of course you are. That's pretty normal under the circumstances. You've been through a tough time, but everything's going to be fine now.'' He smiled, his teeth white and perfect against the perfect tan. It was an easy smile, one that was, she thought, frequently given. Cole's smiles had been infrequent and, like rare gems, dazzling and valuable when unearthed.

She had to quit thinking about him. With every second that passed, every inch of pavement that disappeared beneath the wheels of Geoffrey's car, Cole was retreating into her past. He'd said the past was gone and the future unknowable. Only the present existed, and her immediate present consisted of Geoffrey, not Cole. All she had left of Cole was the memory of their time together.

No, she thought, as Geoffrey exited the freeway. That wasn't right. A memory wasn't all she had of Cole. She also had the strength he'd imparted to her. That strength had enabled her to leave with Sloan, and she couldn't let it slip away now. She had to be strong enough to face her past and her problems, however bad they might be.

Cole had said she didn't have to go with Geoffrey, that she could stay with him until she *got on her feet*. She'd wanted desperately to remain with him but not for the reasons he'd asked her to. She wanted Cole to love her the way she loved him, to want her in his house and in his bed because of that love, not because he felt responsible for her or wanted to help her *get on her feet*.

Whatever happened, she could and would take care of herself, starting now.

Geoffrey drove to the area where she and Cole had distributed posters on Sunday and pulled into an underground parking garage. Jessica had to fight the sudden dizziness of claustrophobia, of the concrete walls, ceiling and floor closing in on her, trapping her. The feeling worsened and she had trouble breathing as they rode the elevator to the fifth floor, walked down the narrow hallway and entered the condo.

The living room was spacious and luxurious. A hunter-green sofa with green and maroon throw pillows dominated the area. Coordinated drapes and wall hangings suggested a professional decorator. The sand-colored carpet sank beneath her feet then bounced back without a trace of her footprints.

The place was beautiful and rich and Jessica hated it. More than anything in the world, she wanted to be back in Cole's big house, feeling Cole's warm breath on her neck instead of Geoffrey's.

Geoffrey locked the door then put the key in his pocket. Jessica's gaze was drawn to that double-keyed dead bolt. For some reason, it didn't look right.

Geoffrey interrupted whatever train of thought was developing when he wrapped his arms around her from behind. It was much the same position as Cole had done last night, but the effect was completely different. Rather than feeling she fit there perfectly, rather than her blood stirring with desire, she felt suffocated, her blood racing with panic.

"Why don't you go freshen up, relax, and we'll have dinner sent in tonight?" Geoffrey suggested.

He guided her down a short hallway and through the door to a large room with dark, heavy furnishings and a four-poster king-size bed covered with a hunter-green spread. It was the gloomy, forbidding room she'd remembered when she'd first opened the door to Angela's bedroom.

She bit her lip and told herself she was being silly. Even though the room wasn't bright and open like the bedrooms at Cole's house, she had no reason to fear it.

However, her heart jumped into her throat as she looked at that bed. Had she shared it with Geoffrey? If they were engaged, they were undoubtedly lovers. Would he expect her to share it again tonight? She couldn't, not after spending last night in Cole's arms.

She turned to face Geoffrey. "Are we...do we share this room?"

He lifted a hand to cup her cheek. "My room is across the hall. We agreed to wait until after marriage. You're a wonderfully old-fashioned girl. That's one of the things I loved about you, your purity and innocence."

Jessica flinched. Though she couldn't remember, she felt certain Cole had not been her first lover. Had she lied to Geoffrey? Or was this something he'd assumed?

And she would have to tell him before they married.

If they married. How could she possibly stand before God and her friends and promise to love, honor and cherish one man when she loved another?

"Geoffrey, we need to talk about the wedding."

He held up one hand. "I know your beautiful dress is ruined, but that's okay. I understand how stressed you were over the plans for a big wedding. I should have realized at the time it was too much for you in your condition. We'll just have a quiet civil ceremony tomorrow."

The panic swelled higher, washing over her in cold waves. "Tomorrow? We can't get married tomorrow!"

He smiled and laid a finger over her lips in a silencing gesture. "Of course we can. I have connections. A couple of phone calls to the right people and we'll be all set. You have yourself a long, lazy bubble bath, put on one of your pretty outfits instead of those jeans, and don't worry about a thing. I'll take care of everything.''

He left the room, closing the door behind him. Jessica heard the well-oiled lock slip into place with barely a whisper.

Chapter Twelve

Cole entered his house and closed the door. No point in locking it or setting the alarm. He could no more lock out the emptiness than he'd been able to lock out the demons that had tormented first Angela and then Jessica.

For the last three years he'd passed through this empty house on the way to work or to bed, not really living here, avoiding the memories of Angela and Billy, and now he had one more to avoid. The place had become full to overflowing with emptiness.

He should call a Realtor tomorrow and put the house on the market, get rid of it and find himself a small apartment somewhere. He probably should have done that three years ago.

The drapes in the living room were open, as he normally left them. There was no one outside to look in, but today he didn't want to look out. He strode over and closed them.

He hadn't meant to linger in the living room, but the bittersweet memory of Jessica curled in one corner of the sofa held him in its grip. Her floral scent still lingered on the air and he'd stood just over there last night, holding her in his arms, feeling her heart beating against his hand.

Damn!

He clenched his jaw and headed determinedly to his office. He'd put aside work the last few days to concentrate on Jessica's case and now was a good time to start catching up. He flopped down in his chair, hit the button to turn on his computer and took an active client file from his desk drawer while the machine booted up.

But he couldn't seem to focus on the documents in the folder. All he could think about was Jessica…the way he'd held her, touched her, made love to her, let her slip in under his defenses…the way that damn Sloan, a man he had no reason to hate but did, had taken her, and the way Cole had let her down.

Logically he knew he hadn't let her down. He'd taken care of her until Geoffrey Sloan arrived on the scene to reclaim his bride. He'd put up the poster that led to Geoffrey's finding her. He'd helped reunite her with her fiancé.

Still he'd let her down. She'd left him as broken and wounded as when he found her. She hadn't recovered her memory. In fact, she'd had a relapse…putting Angela's journal on her bed then forgetting it. And even worse, she'd heard voices.

Jessica was a troubled woman, so troubled she'd had to forget her past.

He recalled his worry that she'd witnessed a murder, and the killer was looking for her. Actually, he'd have preferred that to the explanation of a neighbor boy's injured nose being the source of the blood on her gown. There would have been a good chance—a damn good chance—that he could have protected her from a flesh-and-blood murderer.

But against phantoms in the night, voices from no-where and holes in her memory he had no defenses.

No more defenses than he had against the giant hole her going had left in his life.

Everything felt wrong, badly wrong. But he knew that was just his heart talking. Things were actually right again. Jessica was back with Geoffrey. She was slowly regaining her memory. And he was once again alone.

Except alone had never felt so lonely before.

That night when he went upstairs to bed, he chose the big bed he'd once shared with Angela. Making peace with her memory was much easier than sleeping in the bed where he and Jessica had made love.

Even so, sleep did not come easily. The feeling that something was wrong continued to nag at him.

He'd watched helplessly as Angela's fears worsened until they completely destroyed her. But Jessica had become stronger even in the short amount of time they'd been together. She'd eagerly accepted his offer to teach her self-defense so she could take care of her-self. What had happened to cause her relapse, to cause her to tear a page from Angela's journal and then forget about doing it, to hear voices?

JESSICA AWOKE with a start, heart hammering against her ribs, panic in total control. For a moment she didn't know where she was, only that she didn't want to be there.

She scuttled out of bed and started for the door, then remembered.

The door was locked. She was in the condo with Geoffrey.

Sinking onto the side of the bed, she laid her head

in her hands and took in great gulps of air, ordering herself to relax, talking herself down from the panic attack.

Everything was fine. Geoffrey had locked the door to her bedroom for her own good, so she couldn't run away again or do something crazy, as she'd done at Cole's house, running out into the night with a butcher knife. She had no reason to feel terrified, trapped and suffocated by Geoffrey's actions. She should feel safe and protected.

But the awful truth was, she resented Geoffrey's presence in her life, and that wasn't right. She had an obligation to him. It certainly wasn't his fault she'd run away, developed amnesia and fallen in love with another man. Geoffrey was the victim in all this.

The reason she didn't want to be with him was that she wanted to be with Cole.

And that was not a valid reason to resent Geoffrey.

But it was a valid reason to cancel this hasty marriage he was planning.

She rose from the bed and went into the bathroom to shower. As soon as Geoffrey unlocked that door, they were going to have a talk.

The bathroom was stocked with everything imaginable, from several varieties of perfumed shower gels and lotions to a hair dryer and curling iron, with an entire line of styling products and a basketful of cosmetics. All the items appeared to be new or almost new.

After showering, she went to the closet to select an outfit. Like all the items in the bathroom, the clothes looked new. Apparently she'd brought nothing of her own with her. Geoffrey must have taken her on a shopping spree when they arrived.

She'd just finished dressing in beige linen slacks and a matching silk blouse when the lock on the bedroom door swung open and Geoffrey walked in. He wore slacks and a sport coat with the neck of his white shirt open and carried a silver tray with a steaming cup of coffee, a croissant and a banana. "Good morning, sweetheart," he said. "I didn't expect you to be up so early. Would you like breakfast in bed or in the dining room?"

She surveyed the polished tray with its meager offerings. *Neither,* came the involuntary thought. She wanted to be back in Cole's big kitchen eating a hearty breakfast of bacon, eggs and biscuits.

"I'd prefer the dining room," she replied, suddenly anxious to get out of the enclosed, oppressive space of the bedroom.

Geoffrey smiled approvingly. "That's my good girl."

The words and his paternal tone hit a discordant note in Jessica. If that was the way their relationship had been before her accident, no wonder she couldn't accept him as her future husband.

Although, considering how terrified and lost she'd felt when she woke up on the street in front of Cole's car a few days ago, she could understand why she might have been drawn to Geoffrey at one time. Perhaps after her parents' death she'd needed that substitute for paternal guidance.

But things had changed a lot since then.

She'd changed a lot.

She and Geoffrey walked silently through the condo to the polished ebony table that almost filled the dining niche. A waist-high room divider with carved posts to the ceiling separated the area from the small, galley-style kitchen.

Jessica's gaze was drawn to that kitchen, to the hunter-green countertop, its immaculate surface cluttered only by four maroon canisters and a set of knives in a wooden storage block. The handle of the largest knife seemed to protrude much higher than the others, to beckon her, and she could almost feel the cool solidity of the wood as her hand wrapped around it.

"Jessica?"

Geoffrey's voice jerked her back to reality. He held a chair for her to sit, a chair that would put her with her back to the kitchen.

She slid into the chair gratefully. What was it with her and knives?

As she buttered and nibbled the croissant then sipped the coffee, she avoided looking at Geoffrey across the table. The croissant was not fresh, and the coffee, in spite of the sugar and a strong flavor of hazelnuts, was bitter. She added more butter to the bread and another spoon of sugar to the coffee.

The sounds of silverware on china and cups clinking into saucers rang loudly in the silent rooms.

"I've made some phone calls," Geoffrey said. "If everything works out, before the day's over, you'll be my wife."

Her cup clattered into her saucer as she looked up in horror. "Geoffrey, I told you last night, we can't do that! I'm just starting to get back my memories. This time yesterday I didn't even know my own name!"

He frowned. "I'm aware you have problems, but we love each other, and that's all that matters."

His tone, his entire demeanor, expressed disapproval,

and she wanted to back down, avoid the subject of their impending marriage, hope it would go away.

But it wasn't going away. She had to deal with it.

"I can't marry you. I barely remember you." She swallowed hard. "I don't love you."

His frown deepened. "I wish you wouldn't say things like that. I'm trying to be understanding about your problems, but that really hurts when you say you don't love me."

She clasped her hands on the tabletop. "I know I must have loved you at one time, but I don't remember it."

"That doesn't matter. Even if you never remember what we had before, you'll learn to love me again. As soon as we're married, I'll be able to take care of you. You won't ever have to worry about your problems again."

"That's another thing. I don't even know what my problems were."

"You fell apart after your parents died. You were very depressed."

"Of course I was depressed. Who wouldn't be under those circumstances?" She leaned forward intently, desperately. "Geoffrey, whatever I did, I have to know!"

He folded his napkin and placed it carefully beside his plate. "There's absolutely no reason for you to know things that can only hurt you. We're together again and everything's going to be fine now."

"Stop treating me like I'm a child!" Tears of frustration sprang to her eyes.

Geoffrey's features softened. He rose and came around the table to her. "Now see what you've done? You've upset yourself again." He massaged her neck.

"You're all tense. Finish your coffee. I made it just the way you like it. I'll take care of the dishes while you rest."

"Rest? We just got up."

But she *was* tired.

She lifted her almost-full cup. Maybe the caffeine would give her some energy.

The phone rang and Geoffrey went to answer it.

Jessica felt an enormous sense of relief when he left the room. As if a weight had been lifted from her, she sprang out of the chair, gathered up the dishes and took them into the kitchen, where she poured her coffee down the sink. The extra sugar had made it too sweet but still failed to disguise the bitter taste. If this had been the way she liked her coffee before, she had definitely changed a lot.

She started to load the dishwasher, but the knives again caught her eye, especially the largest one.

As if guided by a force outside herself, her hand moved toward that knife, her fingers wrapped around the handle, and she pulled it from the wooden block.

"That was Judge Robards. We're all set for one o'clock this afternoon."

She whirled to see Geoffrey standing in the doorway and for an instant she thought she saw blood on his left side.

His face contorted with fury as he rushed toward her.

Something clattered on the tile floor and she realized the knife had fallen from her nerveless fingers.

Geoffrey snatched it up with one hand and grabbed her arm with the other, yanking it roughly. "So it was all another one of your lies! You don't have amnesia at all, do you?" He punctuated the sentence with another jerk.

"Stop it! You're hurting me!"

His gaze searched her face for a moment. "I think you need to lie down and rest until it's time for our wedding. You're having another one of your spells."

"My spells?" she repeated, cold fear washing over her. "What do you mean?" The fear drew icy fingers down her spine. "I stabbed you, didn't I? There was no boy from next door with a nosebleed. I stabbed you. That's where the blood came from." With her free hand she reached for his left side, where she'd had the vision of blood.

"No!" He tossed the knife aside and grabbed her hand, pulling it away from his body, but not before she'd felt the roughness of sutured skin beneath his shirt.

"Oh, Geoffrey! What did I do?"

Even as she asked the question, she remembered the sensation of plunging the knife into his flesh, the coppery smell of the blood that soaked through her wedding gown to her skin.

The world around her disappeared and she staggered beneath the weight of the onrush of memories... unlocking the front door with trembling fingers, running down five flights of stairs, terrified at every moment that Geoffrey would come after her, handcuff her again, lock her in the bedroom.

He'd had to handcuff her because she'd tried to kill him!

No, that wasn't right. He'd handcuffed her before she attacked him.

But that made no sense. Had she done something horrible even before that particular attack?

"Jessica, you need to go to your room."

She shook her head, trying to clear it, to focus on

the man standing in front of her, still gripping both her arms. "Just give me a minute to think."

"You can do that in your room where you can't hurt anybody." He tugged, pulling her toward the bedroom. "I've been very patient with you, Jessica, but my patience is wearing thin."

"I'm sorry," she apologized, though she wasn't sure what she was apologizing for.

He led her through the bedroom to the closet and opened the door then yanked out a blue silk dress. "You can wear this for our wedding. White's no longer appropriate for you, anyway, is it?"

She gasped at his insinuation. She hadn't told him about Cole and her making love. How could he know?

"I'm not stupid," he said as if in answer to her unspoken question. "The light never came on in your room after he carried you up those stairs. I know where you spent the night." His smooth voice was rough, almost as if it belonged to another person. His eyes blazed, and his face was red with fury, the face of a stranger. "I wasn't surprised. Not after the way you kissed him and the way you let him touch you when you were outside wearing nothing but that slutty-looking gown. You never let me touch you that way! I thought it was because you were saving yourself, but I was wrong about you, wasn't I?"

"You were watching!" Her head spun as the image of him skulking around Cole's house blended with images of him skulking around her apartment building, waiting half-hidden behind a tree when she came home from dinner with a friend, appearing out of nowhere when she left the building to go shopping.

He grabbed her shoulders and shook her roughly. "I

read what you wrote in that journal about being Cole's wife! Well, you're not his wife! You're mine!''

She hadn't torn that page from the journal then forgotten it. Geoffrey had been in her room. He'd thought Angela's entry was hers. ''That wasn't my journal! I didn't write that! Cole's wife wrote that!''

In another sudden mood change, he kissed her forehead gently. ''No more lies, sweetheart. You take a nap. I'll bring your lunch at eleven so you'll have plenty of time to dress before our wedding.''

He released her and turned to walk away, but she darted after him and grabbed his arm. ''Geoffrey, you can't want to marry me when you know about Cole and me!''

He smiled benignly. ''I know you've been very sick and you're not responsible for your actions. Because I truly love you and I know you love me, I forgive you, no matter how grave your sin.''

Those who truly love will always forgive no matter how grave the sin.

''That was you on the telephone and in my room!''

He took her hand between both of his. His eyes were feverish with the glow of madness. ''I had to let you know that you could come home and all would be forgiven. I admit, I was pretty upset with you when you showed your appreciation for all the things I've done for you by hurting me and running away. But I kept reminding myself of how ill you've been. Do you know what kind of strings I had to pull to get a doctor to help me without reporting you and getting you in trouble?''

''That's why there were no records of a stabbing at any of the hospitals!''

''I had to protect you. How would it look if people

knew my wife had stabbed me? I've tried to take care of you since that first day I met you. You looked so sad and helpless and beautiful sitting there in that restaurant with your friends. I fell in love with you at first sight. You needed me and I promised you I'd always be there. But sometimes you make it awfully hard for me to help you."

She pulled her hand from his and backed away in horror as his words brought memories crowding the edges of her mind, memories she wasn't sure she wanted to own again but knew she must.

Geoffrey wasn't her fiancé. He was her tormentor.

The parts of her life she hadn't yet recovered involved him. Those were the parts she would just as soon never remember, the parts that had induced her amnesia in the first place.

Now they were coming back too clearly. He'd kidnapped her, handcuffed her and brought her to Dallas in the back of his van. When he'd forced her to try on the wedding gown he'd bought, she'd stabbed him and run for her life.

"Get some rest now," he advised, taking her arm and gently guiding her toward the bed where he sat her down.

"Geoffrey, since you know I made love with Cole, you can't possibly want to marry me."

"What you've done doesn't matter. I took care of that man you went to visit who had your pictures all over his house. I cleansed you of his touch. I can do it again."

"The man who had my pictures? You mean Sam? *You* murdered Sam? I never even met the man!"

"He defiled you. Tonight I'll get rid of Grayson and

then you'll be pure again. Our wedding night will be just like we've always planned."

Geoffrey had murdered Sam and now he planned to murder Cole! The horror rang through her mind, paralyzing her so that she made no move to stop Geoffrey from leaving the room. He closed the door, and she heard the *snick* of the lock.

Fear, a dreaded but familiar acquaintance, wrapped dark arms around her as she stared at the closed door. She could understand why she'd wanted to forget Geoffrey, erase the awful events from her mind, but if she'd remembered sooner, she wouldn't be here, trapped in the same situation as before.

Her sanity and Cole's life wouldn't be in danger.

Chapter Thirteen

Jessica sat for several moments, numb with shock and paralyzed with helplessness.

Slowly the realization dawned that this wasn't quite the same situation after all. In recovering her lost memories, she'd returned to the place where she'd left off, but she no longer belonged there. With Cole's presence in her life, she'd changed over the last few days.

The first thing she had to do was calm down and assess the situation.

Geoffrey could hold her prisoner, but he couldn't force her to marry him. When the judge got there, she'd tell him her story. Even if he didn't believe her, even if he thought she was mentally ill, surely he wouldn't perform a wedding ceremony when the bride was unwilling.

Was Geoffrey so insane he actually thought she'd agree?

However, she realized with increasing horror, he might have tried to make sure of her cooperation by drugging her coffee. She recalled feeling tired at breakfast, and then Geoffrey had suggested she take a nap.

He'd drugged her to kidnap her, and the taste of the coffee he'd brought her then had been bitter as it had been this morning. He had access to street drugs. He'd bragged about meeting dealers during ride-alongs with his cop buddies.

She shivered at the thought of what substance she'd just taken into her body.

That's why he hadn't bothered to handcuff her and why he kept telling her to rest; he'd assumed the drug would put her to sleep or at least keep her docile. Thank goodness she had poured most of that awful coffee down the sink.

She sat up straighter. Not only was she not drugged this time, but she wasn't totally helpless either. Cole had taught her self-defense techniques and, more importantly, he'd taught her courage. She'd accepted him into her body and her heart, and she'd absorbed him into her soul.

She checked the one window. Though she was on the fifth floor, if she could tie bedsheets together, she could slide down to safety, but the window refused to open.

She could break it out, but the noise would surely bring Geoffrey running to see what was going on.

In frustration, she slapped the windowsill with the palm of her hand, then hesitated.

Bringing Geoffrey into the room would not necessarily be a bad thing. He'd have to unlock the door and then she'd stand a fighting chance of getting away from him. She'd done it once before, though this time she had no weapon of any sort except her own resources...the techniques Cole had taught her.

But she couldn't really imagine overpowering Geoffrey with what little she knew about self-defense.

She walked over and slumped in the chair, defeated before she even began.

Gradually anger stole over her, replacing the despair…anger at Geoffrey for what he'd done to her, for what he planned to do to Cole, and anger at herself for not being strong enough to prevent any of it.

She *would* break the window and lure Geoffrey into the room. Then she'd make every possible effort to get away from him. If she failed, she'd be no worse off than now, and at least she'd know she'd tried.

She selected a bottle of perfume and a jar of face cream, the heaviest objects she could find, and tossed the perfume at the window as hard as she could.

The resulting noise was all she could have hoped for.

Almost immediately the bedroom door flew open and Geoffrey ran in.

Utilizing the element of surprise, she attacked him with the jar of cream, aiming for his head.

But he stepped aside, resulting in only a glancing blow to his shoulder. Instead of incapacitating him, the pain merely enraged him.

He grabbed her, pinning her arm behind her. "After all I've done for you, this is the thanks I get!"

Though the fear racing through her veins was almost paralyzing in its intensity, she fought it back and focused on remembering what Cole had taught her. Lifting one foot, she slammed the heel against the front of Geoffrey's knee, pushing it backward. Between Geoffrey's curses and her heart pounding so loudly in her ears, she felt rather than heard something snap as he released her and went down.

She'd done it!

She ran for the door, yanked it open and bolted through, down the hall and into the living room.

But when she reached the front door, her heart sank.

Her first impression about the lock being different was accurate. Since the last time, Geoffrey had changed the lock from the standard dead bolt that could be opened from the inside to a double-keyed dead bolt.

And Geoffrey had the key.

She almost wept in her frustration at being so close to freedom and safety only to have it denied her.

She'd have to get the key from Geoffrey.

She turned to head into the kitchen and retrieve the knife again.

But something grabbed her leg and she felt herself toppling.

"You damn bitch!" Using his greater body weight and size, Geoffrey pinned her to the floor.

She struggled, ordering herself not to panic but to think, to focus on reaching his weak spots…the injured knee, his side where she'd stabbed him before. He'd taken advantage of her emotional vulnerability from the time he met her; her only chance was to take advantage of his physical vulnerability now.

She tried to free a hand or leg, but Geoffrey tightened his grip and cursed her. The wildness in his eyes and on his face worsened as his polished veneer completely disappeared, exposing the insanity that had always lurked just beneath the surface.

Suddenly he released one of her arms. Immediately she twisted around, groping for his wounded side, but it was just out of reach of her fingers.

He produced a syringe from his jacket pocket.

The sight of that needle sent more adrenaline pumping through her veins, and she struggled harder, hitting his chest with her free hand. He seemed impervious to pain, cursing her but not backing down in the slightest, even when she got one leg in a position that she could kick his wounded knee.

He struggled to pull back the plunger with his thumb. "Why do you make me do things like this?" he demanded. "If you'd be a good girl, this wouldn't be necessary!"

"I'll be good!" she lied, her heart pounding in terror. "You don't need to do that. Let me up and I'll get dressed for our wedding. We can't get married if you give me that shot." She had no idea what was in the needle and didn't want to find out.

"You're lying! You've always lied to me! I hate liars!"

A pounding on the door stopped them both. "Jessica!"

"Cole! Help me!"

Jessica took advantage of Geoffrey's surprise to push him off her though he immediately lunged after her.

The pounding on the door grew in intensity, becoming loud thuds. "Open up, Sloan! I'll break this damn thing down if you don't!"

"Go away! My wife and I don't want to be bothered!" Geoffrey screamed, grabbing Jessica's arm with one hand while aiming the injection, the plunger now poised and ready, with the other.

Instead of trying to pull away, she swung around and jammed her fingers into his eyes.

He cursed and jerked his head back.

With a final resounding thud, the door flew open.

Cole burst into the room and took in the situation at a glance.

Sloan waved a hypodermic needle in one hand while holding Jessica's arm with the other. Jessica was in a half-crouched position, her eyes wide with fear but her cheeks flushed with adrenaline as she slammed the heel of her hand into Sloan's nose and he released her arm.

In the split second it took for Cole to reach Sloan, he experienced a flash of pride that Jessica was using what he'd taught her.

He delivered a solid punch to Sloan's jaw, causing him to drop the needle, then yanked Sloan upright, twisting one of the man's arms behind his back.

From the corner of his eye, he saw Jessica stagger to her feet.

Sloan turned his head to look at Cole. Even with only that profile view, Cole watched with amazement as Sloan's eyes retreated from their bulging, glowing state and his facial muscles visibly relaxed. His appearance switched from Mr. Hyde to Dr. Jekyll, from a madman to the urbane, polished man he'd met at the police station.

"I'm so glad you're here," he said, squinting through bloodshot eyes, a result of Jessica's self-defense actions. "I was trying to give my wife her medication but she won't take it. You can see how overwrought she is." He smiled sheepishly. "She attacked me. I think my knee may be broken."

Cole ignored him. "Are you all right, Jessica?"

She pushed her hair off her forehead with a shaky hand, but her voice was firm when she answered. "I'm okay."

"What the hell have you got in that hypo, Sloan?"

"Just something to relax Jessica."

"A little Good Time Charley maybe?"

"It's an effective mood enhancer."

"Yeah, in small doses! That's the same thing you gave Sam Maynard!"

"Who?"

"The man you killed. The one who had Jessica's pictures all over his bedroom."

"Oh, him."

"Yeah, him. There's no point in denying it. Somebody saw you coming out of his house." No one had, but Cole figured the bluff was worth a shot.

Geoffrey's placid expression didn't change. "I don't suppose I realized the man had a name," he said negligently. "It's not like he was a real person. Yes, this is the same substance but a much smaller dose. I would never do anything to hurt Jessica. I love her. We're going to be married."

"You're going to spend the rest of your life in prison. Jessica, call 911. Tell them to get somebody over here ASAP and to let Pete know we've got Sam Maynard's murderer."

Jessica moved toward the phone, and Sloan laughed softly. "No, you don't understand. Sam Maynard was a nobody who dared to intrude into my life. I'm somebody, and he's nobody. Eliminating him isn't murder. Jessica, you're going to be very sorry if you make that call. Even if your lover here doesn't know who my father is, you do."

Jessica lifted the receiver. "I know who your father is and I know how much weight he carries. But this isn't Houston and we're not talking about a traffic ticket or a harassment charge. You murdered a man and you kidnapped me. You've terrorized me for the last time." She punched in the three numbers.

"IT'S AMAZING how different all this seems," Jessica said, pausing to look around at the woods surrounding Cole's house as they walked from the garage to the front door. "It's quite beautiful and peaceful now that

Geoffrey's locked up and I know there's nobody lurking behind a tree.''

''You do realize there's a possibility, considering his father's money and connections, that he could make bail and be out in a few days.'' Cole hated to frighten her, but she had to understand the reality of the situation. ''Even if he doesn't, you'll have to testify against him at the trial.''

''If he gets out and comes after me again, I'll deal with that when it happens. But somehow I don't think he will. When he met me, I was grieving for my parents and trying to figure out how to get along in the world without them. I was a victim waiting to happen. He picked up on my weaknesses and knew he could bully me. That's the reason he chose me. Now that I'm stronger, I don't think he'll bother me.''

''How long did you know him before you figured out he was nuts?''

''Not long. Even though I needed guidance at the time, I didn't need somebody trying to run my life. But when I tried to break it off, he refused. He'd be waiting in my apartment with dinner and roses when I got home from work even though I never gave him a key. He interrupted my classes. He'd hang around the parking lot in my apartment complex and follow me if I left. If I protested, he'd go into a red rage.'' She shivered then straightened her shoulders and turned her gaze from the woods around them to him. ''I was terrified of him. But I'm not that same person anymore. I'm looking forward to testifying against him, letting people know the truth.''

Together they continued toward the house.

''I guess he had a lot of people fooled. He puts on a good act.''

She gave a short, bitter laugh. "Yes, he does. When I told my friends I wanted to get away from him, that I was scared of him, they told me I was crazy, that any woman in her right mind would be thrilled to have a man like him…rich, handsome, attentive. And then there were his friends on the police force. I'm sure that's why I didn't trust Pete. The police were allied with Geoffrey."

"His father's influence."

She nodded. "After I changed my lock and got an unlisted phone number then woke up one morning to find that diamond ring and twelve dozen roses in my apartment, I called the police. But Geoffrey had told them we were engaged and that I was having emotional problems after my parents' death. The officers who came out in response to my call told me how lucky I was to have a great guy like Geoffrey. It was a nightmare. Nobody believed me."

Cole unlocked the front door and opened it for her to enter. "They'll believe you now. And after today, I think Sloan knows he can't bully you anymore."

The man had still been complaining about the injuries she'd inflicted on him as the officers hauled him off to jail.

"I had a good teacher." Her gaze was warm, her voice a soft caress.

Cole's blood heated as he recalled the evening he'd shown her the self-defense techniques…the way her body had felt in his arms, the way her heart had pounded against his hand, and the way that tension had finally culminated hours later in the most incredible lovemaking he'd ever experienced. He had to resist the impulse to sweep her into his arms and carry her straight from the front door to his bedroom.

"You were a fast learner," he said, opening the door for her to precede him inside.

As they entered the house, Cole noticed that everything seemed brighter even though the drapes were closed. In the same way the woods now appeared different to Jessica, just so she made his house seem different. The gloom that had been a part of the place since he and Angela moved in lifted with her presence. She even brightened the dark corners.

Or maybe it was just his heart that she brightened.

She went straight to the window and opened the drapes. "What a gorgeous view!"

"Sure is." But he wasn't looking at the view through the window. He was looking at Jessica—at her slender form, her happy smile, the whole of her and the wonder of her. She'd been his for all too brief a time. Now she had her memories and her life back and seemed eager to return to Houston. He didn't blame her. She'd been through quite an ordeal over the last few days.

She'd wanted to go straight to Love Field where Southwest Airlines had frequent flights to Houston. He had talked her into coming home with him to make reservations and be assured of getting on a flight rather than risk waiting hours in the airport. He had talked her into spending one more night with him.

"Have a seat and I'll put on some coffee," he offered.

She grimaced. "I'm not sure I'll ever be able to drink coffee again. I think I'd rather have a cola."

"That sounds good. I'll get us both one."

As Cole left the room, Jessica moved over to sit on the sofa. Suddenly she felt a little uncomfortable. For a few days this house had been home. She'd slept here, showered in the bathroom, felt free to move through the place, to cook meals and clean up after those meals. It had been the only home she'd been able to recall at the time.

For one evanescent moment when she'd walked through the door today, she'd felt as if she were coming home.

But she wasn't, of course. She was a guest, someone who had her own apartment, her own life in Houston, someone who sat on the sofa while the host served drinks.

That was really what she'd always been, a guest in Cole and Angela's home. She'd never belonged here, and now that she could remember where she did belong, she felt out of place.

Maybe she should have gone straight to the airport, not let Cole talk her into coming here. Getting flight reservations instead of taking a chance was the logical thing to do, but the truth was, she'd jumped at the chance to spend a little more time with Cole, possibly even another night in his arms.

Finding the courage to stand up to Geoffrey had been easy compared to finding the courage to face a lifetime without the man she'd fallen in love with.

As if on cue, Cole returned with two red cans of chilled soda and handed her one then sat down beside her. "I set out some steaks to thaw for dinner."

"Sounds good."

He leaned back and put his feet on the coffee table. "I owe you an apology for not believing you about seeing someone outside."

She shrugged and sipped her cola. "I don't blame you. The phone call, the dead rabbit, the figure in the moonlight, and finally those voices in my room had me doubting my own sanity. That's what Geoffrey wanted, of course. I'd become too independent. He wanted me scared and unsure of myself the way I was when he met me so he could control me.''

Cole shook his head. ''I ignored my gut reactions. I let myself be influenced by circumstances instead of what I knew deep inside was the truth.''

''What changed your mind?''

''I didn't sleep much last night. I had a bad feeling that I'd made a big mistake letting you go with Sloan. I kept thinking about those voices you'd heard. I've lived with a woman who was mentally unstable, and you didn't fit the pattern. Along about four o'clock, I decided, by damn, if Jessica heard voices, then somehow voices got into her room. I got up and scanned your room electronically. Found the two microphones Sloan had put there. I didn't know why he'd done it. In fact, at that time, I couldn't even be positive he was the one who'd done it. Except my gut told me he had and that you were in trouble.''

Jessica shuddered as she recalled the events of the morning. ''You were definitely on target on that one.''

He grimaced. ''I was getting a little frantic by the time I finally found the address for that condo. It's in the name of one of his father's companies, so it took me a while. In the meantime, I found the tracking device under the wheel well of my car and realized how he'd located my house.''

''He saw us putting up those posters then followed us to the restaurant and put that tracker on your car while we were eating. He discovered your alarm code through his access to police computers.''

Cole nodded grimly. ''I figured as much. I don't care how much influence his father has, that shouldn't be allowed to happen. Some heads are gonna roll over that one.''

''I hope so. I can't tell you how helpless it made me feel when even the police didn't believe me. I met Geoffrey in March, and by the time the school term ended, I was on the verge of a breakdown. I couldn't eat or sleep. I went to my parents' house in the country to try to escape, but of course he followed me. Gave me some drugged coffee, and when I woke up, I was in the back of his van, handcuffed to one of the seats, heading for Dallas.'' She lifted her arms, exposing the fading bruises on her wrists. ''That's why I didn't want to get into the ambulance. It reminded me too much of that van.''

He took both her hands in one of his and gently stroked the bruises. ''It's a miracle you managed to escape.''

''When we got to the condo, he took off the cuffs so I could try on the wedding gown. By that time, I was pretty hysterical, crying and begging him to let me go. I told him I couldn't marry him, that I didn't love him. That made him furious, and he hit me.'' Her fingers closed around Cole's. ''I started backing away from him, from the living room into the kitchen, and I saw those knives on the counter. I just meant to scare him, but he grabbed me and I—'' She swallowed hard, picked up her soda from the coffee table and took a long drink. ''I stabbed him and ran away,'' she finished. ''I didn't know if he was chasing me or if I'd killed him. I just knew I had to get away.''

''No wonder you didn't want to remember your past.'' Cole's rugged features softened as he spoke. She loved that about him, that he was strong enough to be gentle.

Her gaze swept over his wide chest, the muscular arms protruding from the rolled-up denim sleeves, his big hands holding hers, the knuckles of the right one scraped from the punch he gave Geoffrey. Cole was a strong man on every level.

"Beyond teaching me how to defend myself physically, you gave me the courage to face that past," she said.

He smiled and lifted one hand to trace a finger along her chin. "You always had courage. I saw it that first night. You were terrified but you still had the guts to stand up for yourself, to refuse to get into that ambulance, to make up that awful lie about your name being Mary Jackson and your address being 1492 Main Street."

She laughed. "I've never been any good at lying."

"Neither have I." Cole was suddenly serious. "Well, except to myself. I punished myself for years because I wasn't able to take care of Angela and Billy. I quit a job I loved because I thought I was a failure."

"You weren't a failure! You helped me. Angela had problems that were beyond your control."

"I know. I realized that as I saw you getting stronger and more independent every day. When you told me about the voices in your room, I thought I was wrong, that I'd failed you, too. But then I found the microphones and knew I hadn't. You helped me more than I helped you." He set his feet on the floor and turned to her, his gaze intense but translucent. She could see all the way to his soul, and the demons were gone. "I'm going back to work as a cop," he said.

"Cole, that's wonderful! You'll be much happier, and Dallas will be much safer. I'm so glad you've finally accepted that you really are a capable person."

"It's taken a while to get there. When Pete called to say that Sloan had come to claim you, I thought I didn't have any choice except to let you go with him. I even thought I was doing you a favor, getting you away from me, a man who couldn't take care of you."

"I can take care of myself," she said stiffly. Did he not understand that she was no longer a helpless amnesiac?

"I know you can." He took her soda from her and set it on the table, then clasped her hands in his. "But even before I knew that, even before I found those microphones and realized you could be in danger, sometime in the middle of one of the darkest nights I've ever lived through, I made up my mind to go after you, to fight for you."

The green streaks were back in his dark eyes, a promise of spring, of new life, and Jessica sucked in a quick breath at the intensity of that promise.

"I love you, Mary," he said simply.

The words flowed over her, bringing light and sunshine into her heart and soul, and she wanted desperately to accept them, but he'd called her Mary.

"I'm not Mary anymore. I'm Jessica. I have twenty-six years of memories and hang-ups and habits. I've changed so much over the last few days, I'm not even sure who I am."

"I'm sure. You're the woman I love no matter what your name is or how many memories you have. I love everything about you...your strength and your vulnerability, your body and your spirit. I love the total package whether her name is Mary or Jessica."

Jessica's heart expanded with a warm glow at his words. Cole's hands were still clasped around hers, and she raised them to her lips, pressing a kiss to the scraped knuckles. "I love you, too, Cole Grayson. I think I have from the moment I rolled over in the middle of the street and saw you looking down at me. You seemed so strong and in control but there was so much pain at the back of your eyes."

"You helped me get rid of that pain. This house has always been dark and gloomy ever since Angela and I moved in. When we walked in a little while ago, I noticed how different the place seemed than it had while you were gone. You brighten the dark corners…or maybe it's just that you brighten the dark corners of my heart and it all spills out into the house. I guess it doesn't really matter. I wish you didn't have to leave."

Cole's words brightened the dark corners of Jessica's soul, giving her hope that this wouldn't be their final meeting. "I wish I didn't have to leave, too, but I have a life in Houston, a job, an apartment. I need to take care of my parents' estate, decide what to do with the house and everything in it. I have obligations, but mostly I need to prove to myself that I'm strong enough to make it on my own." Even if she did wish she could spend the rest of her life in Cole's arms.

Cole was silent for a long moment, his gaze holding hers intently. Finally he nodded. "I understand."

Jessica knew she had to do all the things she'd said. She'd barely begun the painful healing and growth process when Geoffrey came along and messed up her life and her mind, but her irrational heart wished Cole had protested just a little. Suddenly fear returned with a vengeance, fear that she would lose Cole.

Even though he'd said he loved her and didn't want her to leave, both their lives would be changing so much while they were apart, she had no assurance that their love would remain constant, that they'd continue to see each other. Even though Dallas and Houston were only forty-five minutes apart by airplane, what kind of a future did they have if they met only on selected weekends? She didn't think she could stand to lose him. No other man could ever make her feel the way he did…warm and protected and excited and completely euphoric all at the same time.

He stood and took her hand, pulling her to her feet and then into his arms. His lips found hers for a slow, searing kiss, and she melted into him.

"I hope you don't plan on getting any sleep tonight," he whispered, his breath warm on her cheek.

She laughed softly. "I'm not the least bit sleepy." For one more night, she would be with Cole. For one more night, he'd hold her and love her. With both their lives changing so much, she had no idea when she'd see him again.

Or *if.*

But tonight she wouldn't think about that. Tonight, she'd savor every moment, storing them in her memory as treasures, no matter what the future might hold.

THE NEXT MORNING Jessica got to the airport only thirty minutes before her flight was scheduled to depart. Though she and Cole had risen early enough, after breakfast, they'd been unable to resist the lure of making love one final time.

Jessica's steps had dragged as she left Cole's house. Would they really be able to continue their relationship with the two of them in different cities? Would they drift apart? Was she leaving his house for the last time?

As they stood in the airport, waiting for her boarding-pass number to be called, Cole held her wrapped tightly in his arms.

"You have my phone number?" he asked.

She smiled. "You gave it to me three times this morning, and I have it memorized. I promise, that's not something I'm going to forget. You have my number and the number at my parents' house. I'll be there most of the time. I've still got to go through and decide what to do with all their possessions."

"Are you sure you don't want me to be with you when you do that?"

"I'm sure I *do* want you with me, but I know it's something I have to do alone." She had to prove to herself—and to him?—that she was strong enough to deal with a traumatic situation. If she and Cole had any chance to remain lovers, they had to be on an equal footing. Yet she found it hard to refrain from asking him to be with her while she sorted through her parents' belongings…to be with her anytime he could or would.

The last group of boarding-pass numbers was called, but still Cole held her body against his and still she made no move to go.

Finally the last few passengers started down the jetway.

"I have to go." She forced the reluctant words up her throat and out her mouth.

"I know." He leaned down and gave her a brief kiss, one appropriate for public display. "I'll call you."

She slipped from his embrace, breaking the connection that gave her life and leaving her feeling alone and cold. She didn't dare look back or she might not be able to do this, would probably run to him, throw her arms around him and beg him to let her stay. Walking away from him was the hardest thing she'd ever done, harder than fighting Geoffrey for her life.

Straightening her shoulders resolutely, she walked toward the jetway that loomed like a dark tunnel leading to her past and her unknown future. If she never saw Cole again, if they drifted apart, if he ceased to be a part of her life, was she strong enough to deal with that? There would never be another man for her. Cole made her heart sing. He made her feel whole. Walking away from him was like walking away from a part of herself.

Handing the flight attendant her boarding pass, she moved on shaky legs toward that tunnel and the uncertainty of her future with Cole.

"Jessica!"

The sound of Cole calling her name sent an immediate surge of happiness through her. She turned to see him standing at the rope that separated the passengers from the others. Unable to resist the chance for one more touch, one more kiss, one more moment with him, she went to him, praying the smile on her face wasn't as bittersweet on the surface as it was inside.

Cole ran a hand through his hair and looked frustrated. "Jessica, I know my timing sucks, but I can't let you go like this."

She opened her mouth to promise she'd be back soon, but he lifted a hand to forestall whatever she meant to say.

"I know you've just survived the engagement from hell," he continued, "and I know this isn't the right time to ask, and I know you've got a lot of things you have to do and you're not ready to rush into anything and I told myself I've waited for you all my life so surely I can wait a little while longer and do this right, but I can't.'' His gaze held hers and she couldn't have moved if she'd wanted to. ''You're being so damn brave about everything, and you think I'm brave, but you're wrong. I don't have the courage to let you leave without doing everything I can to get a promise from you first that you'll come back. For good.''

He took her hand, and the connection she'd lost when she walked away moments before was restored. Just his touch made her feel whole and able to face the unknown future without flinching.

''For good?'' she repeated, a delicious euphoria spreading over her, banishing the darkness. ''You want me to move to Dallas?''

''No. Yes.'' He grinned and shook his head. ''I'm a lot better at bringing in the bad guys than I am at this. Jessica, when you've done whatever you have to do in Houston, will you come back and be a part of my life? I love you. I need you. I don't have the courage to face the rest of my life without you. I want you with me every day and every night. I want you to have my babies. I want us to grow old together. Will you share my life? Will you marry me?''

Jessica could have sworn the sun burst through the roof of the airport, filling her heart as well as the tunnel of the jetway. She could feel a smile spreading across her face. ''Yes,'' she exclaimed. ''Yes, yes, yes! I would love to marry you and have your children and grow old with you. Nothing would make me happier. There's just one thing.''

''I know. You don't want to live in the house I bought for Angela. We'll find a new one.''

''No, that's not it. I don't think Angela would resent my being here. She and Billy have been at peace for three years, and now you are, too. It's up to you. If you want to move, we will. If you want to stay, we will. I don't care where we live as long as I'm with you.''

"Then we'll stay. Two nights ago I slept in the master bedroom, and Angela's ghost was gone. So if that's not it, what is the one thing?"

"Two, actually." She shuddered. "No diamond ring and no formal wedding gown."

He threw back his head and laughed. "We can get married in our blue jeans with cigar bands for rings just as long as you're mine forever."

She smiled and lifted her lips to his. "I can promise you that."

His lips found hers in a kiss that, though it was public and brief, promised a tomorrow filled with joy, of climbing the stairs to bed together and waking up the next morning and all that came between, of children and grandchildren, of all the wonders of being married to Cole.

Epilogue

When the knock came at the front door, Jessica was sitting in the kitchen of her family's farmhouse, drinking a soda and staring out the window at the trees she'd climbed as a child.

For a moment she froze, flooded with a sense of déjà vu of Geoffrey's visit that had resulted in her kidnapping. He was out on bail. Should she have accepted Cole's repeated offers to come down and be with her?

Her hand shook as she set the soft-drink can on the table and pushed herself upright. Briefly she regretted having packed the kitchen knives.

But that was foolish. She couldn't arm herself every time she had a visitor. She couldn't live in fear the rest of her life.

Straightening her shoulders, she walked through the dining room to the living room, past the maze of boxes containing dishes, clothing, sheets, towels...everything that had once been useful or sentimental or treasured by her parents.

The moment she entered the living room, she could see her visitor on the front porch, a familiar figure in blue jeans and a denim shirt.

"Cole!"

A smile stretched across her face and she ran the rest of the way, her feet barely touching the floor, unlatched the screen door and flung herself into his arms. Even though he'd called every day and the sound of his voice had warmed her and eased the pain of saying goodbye to her parents, nothing could take the place of actually seeing him, of touching his solid body, smelling his masculine scent and feeling his arms around her.

She pulled back and looked up, drinking in the sight of his familiar face. "I didn't expect you!"

"I know. I just couldn't wait any longer to see my future wife even though she said she didn't need me."

"I always need you." She lifted her lips to his, and he responded with a kiss that ignited fires in every part of her body. "I think I remember which box the sheets are in," she whispered.

He grinned. "Hold that thought, but first we have to celebrate." He reached down and retrieved a sack from which he took a bottle of champagne. "I've been accepted back on the police force."

"Oh, Cole! That's wonderful!" She hugged him again. "Come inside. I'll unpack a couple of glasses."

"I brought glasses."

He followed her in, and she led him over to sit on the faded sofa that no longer had the colorful afghan her mother had crocheted.

"You've been busy," he observed.

"This room has the boxes with stuff I intend to keep, and the dining room has the ones to go to charity."

He looked around at the stacks of cardboard boxes. "I'm going to guess that this room has a lot more than the dining room. It's a good thing our house has a huge, empty attic!" He grinned and put his arm around her shoulders, pulling her closer.

She smiled sheepishly. "It was hard to decide to let go of anything. It's been hard to let go of my mom and dad and accept that my life has changed forever."

He traced the fingers of one hand along her cheek. "I know," he said softly. "Everything changes, and sometimes those changes are sad, but sometimes they're good."

She captured his hand and pressed her lips to the palm. "You're one of the good changes."

"*We* are one of the good changes."

She snuggled against him. "Yes, we are. And I'm dealing with the other changes." She waved a hand toward the boxes. "Saying goodbye is hard, but it would have been a lot harder if I hadn't been able to talk to you every day and know you were waiting for me."

"Always." He kissed the top of her head.

"But I haven't completely recovered from what Geoffrey did to me. When you knocked, I almost spilled my cola."

"Give yourself a little more time. It's only been a month. I think it's amazing that you've been able to stay down here by yourself so soon. By the way, I found out what happened to the officers who took your call about Geoffrey's harassment and didn't do anything about it."

She flinched. "I hope they weren't fired because of me. They were just fooled by a really good liar."

"The Department of Internal Affairs took your recommendation of a severe reprimand. I think they got off too lightly, but if you're happy, that's all that matters to me."

"I am. I'm very happy. And I'm thrilled about your new job!"

"Then let's begin the celebration." He popped the cork on the champagne and filled two glasses.

"To my future husband, the cop," she said, lifting hers.

"To our new life together."

She started to drink, but he stopped her. "Wait. I forgot something." He set both their glasses on the coffee table, then reached into his shirt pocket and withdrew a cigar band.

Jessica laughed as he took her left hand and tried to place the paper ring on her third finger but tore it in half in the process.

He shook his head. "Oh, man. Do you think that's a sign of bad luck if the engagement ring falls apart?"

She laughed again and kissed him. "No, I do not. We are not going to have anything but good luck from now on. We've both used up our quota of bad for this lifetime."

"I have a backup." He reached into his pocket again and withdrew something that he kept hidden between his thumb and fingers. Again he took her left hand and slid a ring onto her third finger. Though she couldn't see, she could tell by the feel that it was metal, not paper.

Jessica braced herself. She'd told him she didn't want a diamond, but apparently he hadn't taken her seriously. And it was okay. This diamond was from Cole, the man she loved more than life itself. It had nothing to do with Geoffrey, and she wasn't going to get upset about it. Even if she did have a bad reaction, she'd get over it, and Cole would never know.

He moved his hand from hers and she looked down.

A brilliant emerald sparkled on her finger.

"You said no diamonds. I hope you like emeralds."

Happy tears sprang to Jessica's eyes. "I love emeralds! I love you!" She threw her arms around him.

He returned the embrace. "Now let's have that toast...to the beginning of the rest of our lives."

Jessica lifted her glass with her left hand. The glittering gem mirrored the green in Cole's eyes.

They drank a sip, then he pulled her to him, his lips finding hers in a kiss that was familiar yet brand new, a kiss that spoke of the memories they'd already created and all the memories they'd be creating in the future. Those were memories she'd keep forever, stored right beside Cole's love.

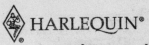

#1 *New York Times* bestselling author

NORA ROBERTS

brings you more of the loyal and loving,
tempestuous and tantalizing Stanislaski family.

Coming in February 2001

The Stanislaski Sisters

Natasha and Rachel

Though raised in the Old World traditions of their
family, fiery Natasha Stanislaski and cool, classy
Rachel Stanislaski are ready for a *new* world of love....

*And also available in February 2001 from
Silhouette Special Edition, the newest book in the
heartwarming Stanislaski saga*

CONSIDERING KATE

Natasha and Spencer Kimball's daughter Kate turns her
back on old dreams and returns to her hometown, where
she finds the *man* of her dreams.

Available at your favorite retail outlet.

Silhouette®

Where love comes alive™